"Do you know any reason why someone wanted your husband dead?" Carlucci asked.

"Not off the top of my head. He was a politician. Politicians tend to have enemies. You'd need to speak to his secretary."

Slipping her arm around her son, she was in the process of squatting down to his height when Carlucci gave a shout: "Sniper."

Before she could even shift her gaze to look at her bodyguard, she was tackled by a hard-driving body, taking both her and Mikey to the ground. She cried out as the kitchen window exploded and something passed within inches of her head to embed itself in the island cabinet.

Another bullet slammed into the floor beside Mikey.

Shock dulled the pain of impact and made her mind grapple to make sense of what was happening. Someone was shooting at them.

Books by Terri Reed

TERRI REED

At an early age Terri Reed discovered the wonderful world of fiction and declared she would one day write a book. Now she is fulfilling that dream and enjoys writing for Love Inspired Books. Her second book, *A Sheltering Love,* was a 2006 RITA® Award finalist and a 2005 National Readers' Choice Award finalist. Her book *Strictly Confidential,* book five of the Faith at the Crossroads continuity series, took third place in the 2007 American Christian Fiction Writers Book of the Year Award, and *Her Christmas Protector* took third place in 2008. She is an active member of both Romance Writers of America and American Christian Fiction Writers. She resides in the Pacific Northwest with her college-sweetheart husband, two wonderful children and an array of critters. When not writing, she enjoys spending time with her family and friends, gardening and playing with her dogs.

You can write to Terri at P.O. Box 19555, Portland, OR 97280. Visit her on the web at www.loveinspiredauthors. com, leave comments on her blog at www.ladiesofsuspense. blogspot.com or email her at terrireed@sterling.net.

THE
INNOCENT
WITNESS

Terri Reed

Love Inspired

Recycling programs
for this product may
not exist in your area.

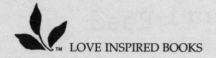 ™ LOVE INSPIRED BOOKS

ISBN-13: 978-0-373-67469-5

THE INNOCENT WITNESS

Copyright © 2011 by Terri Reed

www.LoveInspiredBooks.com

Printed in U.S.A.

God is our refuge and strength,
a very present help in trouble
—*Psalms* 46:1

Thank you to my editors
at Love Inspired Suspense, Emily Rodmell
and Tina James. I so appreciate all you do.

ONE

One o'clock in the morning.

Her son's bed was empty. Anxiousness jump-started Vivian Grant's frozen blood.

"Mikey?" she called out as she frantically searched her eight-year-old's closet, under the bed and in the connected bathroom. Empty.

A thud had awoken her.

This wouldn't be the first time he'd tried to escape the house in the middle of the night.

The locator monitor!

She raced back to her room and groped for the wall light switch, then flipped it on. A soft glow filled the room, casting shadows on her antique four-poster bed. The Wanderer Alert receiver sat atop her dresser. She grabbed it. The locator screen showed that Mikey or at least the ankle bracelet he wore was still within the set parameters of the house. She wouldn't breathe a sigh of relief, though, until he was in her arms. Palming the device, she ran downstairs.

Searching all his normal hiding spots proved fruitless. Not in the kitchen. Not the living room or the playroom. She passed the empty dining hall and hurried toward her husband's quarters. Had Mikey gone to see his father?

A normal desire for any eight-year-old boy, even one with autism.

In her head, she could hear Steven's snarled complaint that she couldn't control her son. Mikey had stopped being *their* son the minute they'd received the autism diagnosis.

She clenched her fist as she entered her husband's sacred domain. For more years than she could remember this part of the house had been off-limits to her and Mikey. Steven liked his privacy. But mostly he didn't want anything to do with them, his family. Except when it served his burgeoning political career.

Steven's sitting room was empty. So was the bedroom. His bed was still made up. She flipped on the light in the connecting bath. No one. Where were they?

A horrible thought streaked across her mind. Had Steven finally had enough and taken Mikey to a home? Every time Steven perceived some offense on her part, he yanked her chain with the threat.

The very idea of losing Mikey choked her with rage and fear.

Dread slithered through her veins. Steven had seemed even more furious than normal earlier because Mikey had interrupted his dinner by throwing a fit when a baseball game preempted his favorite television show. She'd chalked up Steven's overreaction to his campaign heating up. Election time always increased the stress around their home.

No. He wouldn't send Mikey away, she rationalized. If he did, what would Steven have left to hold over her?

Smoldering anger and terror spurred her toward Steven's study. Light leaked from beneath the door. Steven hated when she came to his study uninvited, but right now she didn't care. She'd put up with his wrath for her son. She flung the door open. Her gaze swept the room. No Mikey. Her heart sank.

Steven sat at his desk, his chair twisted away from her so she could only see the top of his salted dark head over the high back of his red leather chair. Working, as usual.

"Steven, have you seen Mikey?"

Steven didn't respond. Annoyed at being ignored yet again, she rounded the chair and sucked in a sharp breath. Steven's head lolled back, his eyes open and unseeing. A large ornamental knife—the knife she'd bought him for their first anniversary while on a trip to China—protruded from his chest. A crimson stain spread over his white dress shirt.

Shock siphoned the blood from her brain. The world tilted. Her knees buckled. She clutched the desk to keep from hitting the floor. A sob escaped.

She reached out with a shaky hand and pressed two fingers to the spot where his pulse should beat. Nothing.

Revulsion and horror swept through her. Someone had violently murdered Steven. In their home.

Panic gripped her heart. Where was Mikey? He had to be here. *Please, Lord,* she prayed, trying not to lose complete control. "Mikey?"

Eerie silence settled around her, sending chills down her spine. Nearly hysterical, she grabbed the phone and fumbled to dial 911. It seemed to take forever for the emergency operator to answer. "What is your emergency?"

"My son!" A sob broke through. "Someone's taken my son and…killed my husband, Senator Grant."

* * *

From deep in the shadows of a blooming cherry tree growing near the patio of the Grant's Woodley Park home, the man watched Vivian Grant through the study window with interest. He'd barely made it out the sliding door before she'd burst into the room.

He hadn't thought he and Steven had made enough noise to draw her attention. But there she was, looking beautiful as usual. Even in the middle of the night, Viv was a sight to see. All curves beneath her silky pajamas, her long blonde hair cascading down her back, her big blue eyes filling with tears. Her pretentious mother had known what she was doing when she'd named the future beauty queen after the *Gone with the Wind* movie star.

Steven hadn't deserved such a woman. He'd come from nothing and ended up with everything. Or at least he'd thought he had.

The upstart had had the nerve to try blackmailing him. Ha!

He'd shown Steven Grant just what he thought of the extortion threat. He hadn't come here tonight with murder on his mind. He'd come expecting to reason with Steven. But no go. The idiot wouldn't listen.

Steven really should have heard him out. Now it was too late.

Frustrated rage had overtaken his good sense. The decorative knife sitting on the mantel had been within arm's reach. And years spent throwing knives at birch trees as a boy had made wielding the knife too easy. His fists clenched. Grant had driven him too far.

And now he couldn't search for the evidence Steven had claimed to have.

He saw Viv pick up the phone. Calling for help, no doubt. Time to leave and act properly shocked when news of the murder became public knowledge.

He'd make arrangements for the premises to be searched tomorrow.

As he began to turn away, movement inside Grant's home office froze him in place.

A thin, young boy, clutching a teddy bear, climbed out from beneath the massive mahogany desk. Viv dropped the phone as she sank to her knees and gripped the boy tight.

The man gritted his teeth. How had he not known the child was there? Steven must have been protecting the kid.

And the brat could possibly identify him.

Viv lifted her head, her gaze boring straight

at him through the window. He jerked back farther into the shadows. Logically he knew she couldn't see him, she couldn't know he was here. Didn't matter. She and the child both posed a threat that would need to be removed. Quickly.

As he left the scene, he plotted the best way to eliminate Vivian Grant and her son, Mikey.

Relief flooded through Viv as she clung to her son. "Thank you, Lord."

She placed a kiss on Mikey's bent head, breathing deep the scent of powder-fresh shampoo clinging to his dark curls. Quickly, she checked to see that he was unhurt. His thin shoulders bowed inward as he hugged his tattered bear to his chest and his pj's hung on his small frame, but he didn't appear injured.

She lifted his chin with her finger and tried to make eye contact. His midnight-blue eyes looked everywhere but at her. Not unusual even in the best of circumstances. Focusing on personal interaction took energy and concentration. "Mikey, what are you doing down here?"

"Daddy." The single word came out whisper-soft. He dropped the bear. His right hand grasped his left index finger and began to twist, the skin growing red with the exertion. A sign of his growing agitation.

"I know, baby, I know." She needed to get him out of the room and away from the macabre scene.

Was the killer still in the house? Could she and Mikey make it to the secret passageway in the dining room that came out next to the detached garage?

The distant wail of a siren filled her with relief. The police would handle this. They'd protect her and Mikey.

Taking Mikey by the arm, she urged him toward the study door. The quicker they got to safety the better.

He dug in his heels. "Bear!"

She scooped up the stuffed toy. "Come, sweetie. We need to go."

She ushered him swiftly toward the front door. Decorum dictated she stop at the entry-way closet long enough to grab a long wool coat to cover her pajamas. She slipped on a pair of rain boots, the only footwear available in the closet. Taking Mikey's jacket off the hanger, she slung it over her arm. Figuring she should have her ID on her, she snagged her hobo-style carryall bag from the entry-way table and slipped the monitor and the bear inside before shepherding Mikey out onto the porch.

She knelt beside Mikey and pulled on his coat. "Can you tell Mommy what you saw?"

Could he identify Steven's killer? She held her breath, waiting for Mikey to reveal something. "Mikey? I need you to tell me what you saw."

He abandoned twisting his finger in favor of flapping his hands, a sign that a fit was brewing. Whatever he'd seen was locked up inside his head. Pushing him would only drive him further away.

The loud screech of tires combined with flashing red-and-blue lights sent Mikey into a full-blown agitated fit. He batted at his ears and made a high-pitched noise echoing the siren's wail even after it was turned off. Viv's heart pitched. At the moment she couldn't do anything to help him. He would continue on until the chaos ended. Which might take a while. She kept one hand on his shoulder, more for her comfort than his.

Two police cruisers pulled into the drive-way. Four officers jumped out of the cars.

"Mrs. Grant?" An older officer stepped close as the others hung back.

"Yes. I'm Vivian Grant. I'm so glad you're here."

"Officer Peal," he said, his gaze sliding to Mikey. "We had a call that your son was missing and your husband...killed?"

She nodded. "My son was hiding. His father... Senator Grant is dead." She pointed toward the house. "In the study."

Peal gestured with his head. Two officers entered the house, hands on their holsters. The third officer moved toward the back of the house.

Peal gestured toward the cars. "Ma'am, can I have you and your son take a seat inside my car? Just until we know for sure the scene is secure."

She gestured to the flashing lights on top of the police cars. "Could you turn off the lights first? They're bothering my son."

"Sure thing, ma'am." Peal vaulted down the porch steps to the nearest cruiser. A second later the flashing light went dark.

"Let me take care of the other car," he said as he walked around the front of the vehicle. A moment later the second cruiser's lights went out.

Mikey calmed almost immediately. His

high-pitched whine

per. He went bac

finger.

Viv maneuvered

senger seat of the n

smelled of stale coffe

least it was less cons

on the porch in the s

safer.

The Innoce

as the image of St

"I called 911

as you arr

Pea

18

any

A metal grate separated them from the front seats. Mikey grabbed a hold and shook the metal. The deafening rattle bounced around the interior of the vehicle. Now Viv knew how criminals must feel, like caged animals. A familiar helpless, vulnerable sensation slithered up her spine, reminding her of her childhood.

Taking deep breaths to harness her rising anxiety, she silently repeated in her mind, *This too shall pass*.

Peal squatted next to her, bracing one elbow on the back wheel well, and removed a small notepad from his shirt pocket. His pen poised over the paper. "Ma'am, can you tell me what happened?"

"A noise woke me. I thought it was Mikey needing something. But he wasn't in his bed so I went to ask Steven if he'd seen Mikey. I found Steven… He'd been stabbed." Bile rose

...ven's death filled her brain. *...hen* I found Mikey hiding just *...ved.*"

... nodded encouragingly. "Did you see *...one* else in the house?"

She shook her head. "No."

"Homicide will have more questions for you."

The sound of more vehicles arriving floated into the car through the open door. Viv twisted around to look out the back window. Two men dressed in dark suits climbed out of a black SUV and made their way toward the cruiser. It didn't take a genius to know who these guys were. Viv had seen enough of them during her years as a politician's wife to recognize the swagger of the FBI.

She wasn't surprised the FBI had been called. Steven was a junior senator, after all, and had just declared his intent to run for the presidency.

Mikey drew her attention when he began combing her hair with his fingers. One of his calming rituals.

Officer Peal greeted the two men as they stopped beside the police car. Viv leaned forward to listen.

The men flashed credentials. "I'm Agent Jones, this is Agent Thompson."

"Homicide hasn't arrived yet," Peal said. "I've got two men inside and one searching the perimeter."

Agent Jones slanted a glance at Peal. "Good work, Officer. We'll take care of the witnesses."

Thompson leaned into the open door of the cruiser. His puggish face with round probing eyes sent goose bumps prickling Viv's skin. "Mrs. Grant, we need you to come with us."

"Where?"

He grasped her by the elbow and tugged. "We're to escort you to the WFO."

She stiffened. She didn't like being manhandled. "WFO?"

"Washington Field Office."

"I want to see your badges," she demanded.

Each agent let her inspect their credentials. The official-looking identification appeared in order. She handed them back. "Shouldn't we wait for Homicide?"

"They can question you at headquarters. It's safer this way," Agent Jones supplied as he also reached in to help pull her from the vehicle. He was a big man with a scar on his chiseled chin. She was no match for the two of them.

"All right, already," she snapped and climbed out of the cruiser. "Can I get a change of clothes?"

"No ma'am. No time. We've orders to bring you in ASAP," Jones said.

Feeling self-conscious, she buttoned up her coat and then worked to transfer Mikey from the police vehicle to the SUV. He didn't like strangers touching him either, so Viv had to coax and cajole him along while the two agents urged them to move faster. Their sense of urgency fueled her fears. Surely the agents didn't really believe she and Mikey were in danger now?

Once they were safe and secure inside the SUV, Viv settled back against the black leather seat as an adrenaline crash zapped her energy. The darkened interior calmed Mikey as well. He snuggled against her body, his fingers raking through her long loose hair. She struggled to keep her eyes open as the agents drove them out of her neighborhood.

Lulled by the silence and the smooth motion of the ride, her head nodded. She jerked awake. She needed to stay alert. She scanned the passing scenery. This wasn't downtown. They were headed toward an industrial part of D.C. that was mostly deserted at night. Dread coiled low in her belly and the small hairs on the nape of her neck rose.

"Excuse me, where are we going?" She was sure the FBI had some covert facilities she didn't know about, but this seemed strange.

Neither man answered.

Unease gripped Viv. Her heart raced. "This isn't anywhere near the field office on Fourth Street."

The driver, Agent Jones, replied, "Relax, Mrs. Grant. This will be over soon."

Over soon? That sounded ominous. What was going on?

Anxiety revved along her veins. Were these men Steven's killers and not really FBI agents? Were she and Mikey next? A fresh rush of adrenaline pounded through her heart, making her blood race. She had to do something to protect her son and herself.

Lord, what do I do?

Her bag lay at her feet. She inched down on the seat until her fingers snagged the strap and pulled the bag onto her lap. She cautiously rummaged around inside, careful not to make any noise, until she found the two items she sought. Her small Taser and an ounce-sized bottle of perfume. Steven had thought her foolish for insisting on getting her firearm permit and carrying the miniature protection device. He'd mocked the self-defense classes, as well.

But foolish or not, she'd known being the wife of a politician put her and Mikey at risk.

And her caution was about to pay off.

She readied herself, needing to wait until the vehicle stopped before attempting to disarm her abductors. The last thing they needed was an accident. With her left hand she gripped the seat belt and coughed to cover the noise as she undid the buckle. Agent Thompson, seated on the passenger side, briefly glanced back.

"Tell me what is going on." Viv leaned forward to keep the agent from seeing that her seatbelt wasn't buckled.

"Only following orders, ma'am," the agent said before turning back around.

"Whose orders?"

He ignored her question. Though she hadn't expected a reply, frustration pounded at her temple. She had a bad feeling that their orders weren't in line with hers and Mikey's well-being. If her suspicions were true, these men could very well be Steven's killers and she and Mikey were the next victims.

Panic threatened to consume her. She tamped it down. Mikey needed her. She had to keep a cool head and be ready to act the second she had a chance. She forced the rising fear to the back recesses of her mind.

The SUV left the paved road and rattled down a dirt drive until it rolled to a stop in the gravel lot of a big warehouse. There were no other cars. No people. Her fist clenched the belt as she eased the strap back into its holder.

As soon as the engine died, Agent Jones removed the keys from the ignition and dropped them into the pocket of his suit coat. He opened his door.

Agent Thompson opened the passenger door. Viv tucked the Taser against her leg and readied herself. Both men climbed out of the vehicle.

Viv reached across Mikey to lock the back door on his side just as Jones reached for the handle, the sound of his trying the locked door handle echoed inside her head.

"Mikey, hold your breath, like swimming!" she instructed.

Thompson opened the back door on her side and reached inside for her. "Get out, Mrs. Grant."

"Not on your life." She brought the perfume bottle up just like she'd been taught and gave a short blast, while at the same time planting her foot into the agent's chest and shoving with all her might.

With a scream of surprise, Agent Thompson tumbled back and landed on the ground, wiping at his eyes. Counting on the perfume to keep his eyes watering and him disoriented, Viv pulled the door closed and hit the lock. The air filled with the scent of her expensive perfume. She coughed. One glance at Mikey, his cheeks puffed up with air, assured her he was doing as she asked. She dropped the bottle and palmed her Taser.

"Hey!" Agent Jones reached for his holstered gun and moved to open the driver's side door.

Without hesitation, Viv scrambled between the captain's seats, locking the passenger door before quickly sliding into the driver's seat. Jones made a grab for her. She touched the low wattage mini Taser to his arm.

With a loud oath, he let go of her and stumbled back. His gun fell to the ground.

Viv's instincts told her to grab the door and lock it shut, but what good would that do? They'd be sitting ducks inside the vehicle. Even if the SUV was equipped with bullet-resistant windows or side armor, she and Mikey were as good as done for unless they got away. She needed the SUV's keys.

Praying she'd remember her kicks and

punches from her women's self-defense classes, she jumped out and ran to Jones, who sat on the ground looking stunned. The Taser had done its job—momentarily immobilizing her attacker. Supposedly long enough to run away. But she rushed closer.

He lashed out, his forearm connecting hard against her hip sending her careening sideways. But years of teetering on high heels had taught her to recover her balance quickly. She bent her knees and found her center. Using her elbow, she landed a jab across the agent's jaw. Taking advantage of the moment, she grabbed the keys from his jacket pocket and then practically dove back into the driver's seat of the SUV.

She yanked the door shut, locked it and fumbled with the keys. Jones got his feet underneath him. Frantic, she managed to get the right key in the ignition and start the engine just as he reached the door. He banged on the glass with the butt of the gun, trying to break the glass. Viv flinched. On the other side of the SUV, Thompson had risen, but was stumbling around, still clutching his face.

Throwing the vehicle into reverse, she floored the gas. The SUV shot backward, away from the two agents. She twisted the wheel, sending the big boat of an automobile into a sliding spin. When the nose of the SUV was pointed away from the agents and toward the road, she threw the gearshift into drive and roared away, leaving the two agents in the dust.

In the backseat Mikey grew agitated. He hit his ears and rocked back and forth. She powered down the window to let fresh air in and clenched her jaw tight, hating that she couldn't comfort her son. She had to concentrate on getting them as far away as possible as quickly as possible. Though unfamiliar with the streets in this part of town, it didn't take her long to find her way to a major thoroughfare.

Thirty minutes later, she pulled off the road and parked in the dark lot a of strip mall. She needed help. She knew what she had to do. Making this call grated on her pride and twisted her insides into knots. But for Mikey's sake she would do anything.

Her father was the only one who could help. With trembling hands, she dug her cell phone out, dialed his cell phone and waited anxiously. When her father answered, the relief she felt at the sound of his voice surprised her.

Tears filled her eyes. "Dad, I'm in trouble."

* * *

Anthony Carlucci stared at the brick brownstone nestled halfway down the block on one of Boston's prestigious Back Bay neighborhood streets. Not what he'd expected. He'd imagined the famous Trent Associates to be housed in some state-of-the-art glass skyscraper in a more metropolitan area downtown, not this unassuming brownstone with quaint shutters, window baskets teeming with colorful flowers and stone steps leading to a wide door painted red.

But lately life hadn't turned out the way he'd expected. Why should this be any different?

Just to be sure he was at the right place, he checked the address on the business card his sister Angie had thrust into his hand two days ago when she'd visited the construction site where he worked as night security. Having been in the protection business for years, Anthony had heard of James Trent and his league of personal protection specialists. He'd just never imagined himself becoming one.

"Take one assignment. See how it goes," his sister had said, her big brown eyes imploring him to do as she wanted.

"I don't want to be responsible for other people's lives again," he'd countered, hating the reason his life had been derailed. Guilt and pain ate at him night and day, never letting him forget his failure.

"When are you going to stop wallowing in this ridiculous self-pity?" Angie had demanded, using her best cop voice.

As a Boston homicide detective, she had the art of intimidation down pat. Of course she'd had to learn to stand strong against her two older brothers growing up. And just like their father, a Boston police officer, and both him and their other brother Joe, an ATF agent, she'd gone into law enforcement.

"You don't get to judge me," he'd snapped. Being called on the carpet by his baby sister for his state of mind hadn't sat well.

She'd sighed. "I'm not judging you. I'm worried about you. Just talk to Trent. See what he has to offer. It's got to be better than this." She'd made a sweeping gesture. "*You're* better than this."

He wasn't so sure. The bitter taste he'd had in the back of his throat for weeks intensified.

"You have a law degree. At least do something with that."

"I'm only licensed in D.C." Practicing law had never been his goal.

She'd cut the air with her hand. "Excuses!"

They'd stared at each other for a long moment. Love for his sister filled him. He reached out to give her a hug. He appreciated her concern even if he didn't deserve it.

"Please, pray about it," she'd urged.

He hadn't the heart to confess to his little sis that he and God weren't on speaking terms lately.

But last night he'd finally capitulated and called Trent because self-pity was a cold and nasty companion. And frankly, the job at the construction site didn't pay all that well. Anthony had resorted to living off his credit cards. Not exactly a noble or prudent way to survive.

So here he was on a bright Monday morning, at the threshold of a possible new future. One he hadn't yet decided he really wanted.

The "clickity-clack" of high heels against pavement halted him on the first stair. A man and woman approached and turned down the walkway, clearly headed to Trent Associates. Though Anthony guessed they were both in their late twenties or early thirties, the two couldn't have been more opposite if they'd tried.

The exotically pretty woman dressed in a knee-length black skirt, black formfitting blouse and black pumps was a sharp contrast to the tousled blond man in loafers, khakis and a bright blue polo shirt.

"Can we help you?" the woman asked.

From the way her gaze sized him up, Anthony guessed she was some kind of police officer. Or had been, since Anthony's research showed most of Trent Associates were ex-something-or-other, just like him.

"I have a meeting with James Trent," Anthony replied. He stuck out his hand. "Anthony Carlucci."

"Well, come on in," the man said, grasping Anthony's hand while clapping him on the back. "Wouldn't do to keep the boss man waiting. I'm Kyle Martin and this firecracker is Simone Walker."

Simone shot a hard glare at Kyle, who only grinned before bounding up the stone steps and pushing through the front door of Trent Associates.

Simone shook Anthony's hand. "You'll have to excuse Kyle. He's like a big puppy in need of obedience training."

"I heard that!" Kyle's voice floated out of the open front door.

Simone rolled her dark eyes and preceded Anthony inside. A reception desk sat straight ahead at the bottom of a curved staircase. An olive-skinned woman, with black hair twisted into a knot at her nape and dressed in a red business suit, manned the station. She gave them a wide, welcoming smile. "Morning, Simone."

"Morning, Lisa." Simone replied. "We have a guest. Anthony Carlucci."

"So I see. Good morning, Mr. Carlucci."

"Good morning." Anthony returned the smile but found his gaze drifting, taking in the house-turned-office-space. The entry-way's dark wood paneling, gleaming hard-wood floors and intricate crown molding all spoke of age and wealth. Large antique-looking landscapes adorned the walls. To the right of the front door a set of double sliding doors, popular in the early nineteen hundreds, stood wide open revealing a parlor room dec-orated in rich warm shades of rust and red. Two sofas and several leather chairs created an intimate grouping.

"That's where we interview potential clients," Simone said.

What made her think he wasn't a client?

Kyle appeared in the doorway at the end of the hall. "Anyone hungry? I'm making omelets."

"I've eaten, thank you," Simone said and then looked inquiringly at Anthony, as if offering him breakfast was a normal thing.

Bemused by both the offer and the easy way they treated him like one of their own, he said, "Same."

Kyle shrugged and disappeared back into the kitchen.

Simone smiled revealing dimples at the corners of her mouth. "We're one big happy family."

Not sure how to respond to that, Anthony nodded. Though he'd trusted those he worked with implicitly, he'd never thought of his co-workers as family. "How many associates are there?"

"Ten at present." She gave him a thoughtful look, then gestured to the woman behind the reception desk. "Lisa will let James know you're here."

Lisa picked up the receiver of an old-fashioned telephone. "Anthony Carlucci to see you."

After a pause she said, "Yes, sir."

She hung up the phone and gestured toward the wide staircase leading to the brownstone's upper story. "James is in his office. First door on the right. Go on up."

"Thank you," Anthony said as he watched Simone move toward a closed door farther down the hall. She flashed him a polite smile before going inside. The sound of voices floated down the hall toward him before the door shut behind her.

Interesting people.

Anthony took the stairs and stopped at the first door on the right to knock as directed.

"Come in."

He pushed open the door. The office was spacious, with a bank of windows overlooking the street allowing natural light to fill the room. Seated behind a wide black lacquered desk was the man Anthony had come to meet.

Again Anthony's expectations were blown to smithereens. He'd imagined Trent as a General Patton type. So not the case.

James Trent rose and came around the desk. Average in height with graying temples and laugh lines at the corners of his eyes, his wiry frame exuded energy that fairly cracked around the man. He stuck out his hand and gave Anthony a firm handshake. "So glad your sister convinced you to contact me.

Something has come up that you'll be perfect for."

Anthony blinked. "Excuse me?"

Trent gestured to the leather chair facing the desk. "Take a seat and I'll fill you in." Without waiting for Anthony to comply, James picked up a folder and handed it to him. "Your first assignment."

Anthony hesitated for a fraction of a second before his fingers closed over the file. "Just like that? You don't want to ask me any questions?"

James's gaze turned shrewd. "I know what I need to know. Do you?"

A variety of questions sprang to mind, but Anthony knew the important question wasn't about the pay or the hours.

Was he ready to commit?

Decision time. Go back to his security guard job or step forward into new territory. Maybe if he completed a task more challenging than chasing away vagrants and metal thieves, he'd somehow find his self-worth again and maybe, just maybe, reclaim his life and his dignity. "One assignment."

Or maybe he'd screw up again and feel even worse.

The corner of James's mouth tipped up. "Fair enough."

Heart racing with anticipation, Anthony took a seat and opened the file.

TWO

"Sir, we located Mrs. Grant and her son."

Relief dribbled down the man's back in a rivulet of sweat. He stared out the floor-to-ceiling window overlooking the Potomac River. The afternoon sun danced on the water's surface. In the background the Washington Monument rose like a lone sentinel.

His men had underestimated Vivian. Most people probably did.

He'd never thought Steven gave his wife enough credit. In any other circumstance, he'd applaud her bravery and ingenuity. But her survival threatened his existence. He couldn't allow that. "That's good, Wendell. Send a team to take care of her and the kid. Make sure they don't fail like last time."

"Already done, sir. And I paid off Officer Peal. He won't be a problem."

The eager-to-please note in his assistant's

tone set the man's teeth on edge. He refrained from showing his irritation. "Good."

Now at least Viv's version of the murder would be suspect, if the authorities happened to catch up to her before she could be neutralized.

"I want it clean. No traces back to me."

Wendell looked affronted. "Of course. As always."

The man's lips wrapped around his teeth in a semblance of a smile. "What would I do without you?"

A cagey look flashed across his assistant's normally bland features before being carefully masked into a benign humility. "I couldn't say, sir."

As Wendell retreated out the office door and back to his own desk, the man decided Wendell had become a liability. He knew too much, assumed too much. Once this mess with the Grant woman and her brat was taken care of, it would be time to find a new assistant. They came a dime a dozen. Eager, young grunts willing to do whatever necessary to make the grade.

The man went to the wet bar and poured himself a drink. He was surprised to find his hands shaking as he lifted the tumbler to his lips. Before partaking of the amber liquid, he mumbled, "May you rot in your grave, Steven Grant. And may your lovely wife and son join you very soon."

"Vivian, it's time to get up."

Viv started awake at the sound of her father's deep, gravelly voice. She whipped her head around to find the other half of the bed empty. She'd finally managed to slip into an exhausted sleep after two restless nights and had apparently been out of it enough for Mikey to leave the room.

Panic infused her. She bolted upright. "Mikey?"

"In the living room watching some ridiculous cartoon," Ben LeMar replied with a frown marring his tanned face. "I had some more clothes brought over from the house."

"Mom?" she asked, trying not to grimace as she waited for the reply.

Dad shook his head. "I'd like to keep her out of this for as long as possible. She's upset enough that I've been working here all weekend."

Viv nodded with relief and sent up a short prayer of thanks that she wouldn't have to deal with her mother. The last thing Viv needed was her mother's sharp-tongued criticisms and her needling about Mikey being better off in a specialized facility. Besides, Mom would be the one mourning Steven and no doubt blaming Viv for the tragedy. Viv was so not up for that.

"Has there been anything on the news?" she asked.

"Strangely enough, no. Someone is keeping Steven's death very quiet."

Dad retreated, leaving the bedroom door open. From somewhere in the house she heard the obnoxious sounds of Mikey's favorite show. Outside the bright window covered in gauzy drapes, the sound of hammers and saws filled the air, signaling the beginning of a workweek.

Her stomach twisted. Whoever killed Steven was powerful enough to keep his death out of the media. And send two federal agents to do her harm. Not a comforting thought.

She climbed out of the warm bed. Immediately the air-conditioned air chilled her skin. Her gaze swept the room, taking in her surroundings. Plush beige carpet, coffee-colored walls splashed with colorful artwork, high ceiling sporting a whirring fan light. A fireplace beside an arched doorway separated the room from the bath. All very tastefully appointed.

No doubt her mother's doing. One thing

Lilith LeMar was good at was decorating. Decorating her house. Decorating her only child. Most of the time Viv had felt like her mother's doll rather than her daughter.

Viv's gaze landed on her old pink flowered suitcase sitting on the floor at the base of the bed. Tenderness welled at her father's thoughtfulness. He, at least, did show his love occasionally with his actions if not his words.

After calling her father two nights ago and explaining the situation, she'd followed his instructions and driven to the airport. He'd arranged for two tickets on the first flight out of Dulles to Boise. She'd been terrified they'd be stopped by authorities, but thankfully, they weren't. Her father had been waiting in a dark green Range Rover when they'd arrived. After stopping at the grocery store he'd brought them here, where no one would think to look for them.

"Here" was a nicely arranged model home in a brand new subdivision. Definitely *not* her childhood home, which, though equally well-appointed, was by far grander and bigger and set on a fifty-acre estate on the outskirts of Boise.

Obviously, her father had brought her to one of his investment properties. Along with phosphate mining, her father dabbled in residential construction because he liked building communities.

Probably because there was no community within his own family, Viv thought with a dose of bleakness.

Quickly, she showered and dressed in black slacks, a pink cashmere sweater and silver flats. She wound her wet hair up into a French twist and secured it at her nape with a jewel-studded clip. She touched her lips with pink gloss, swiped a touch of mascara on her lashes and called it good.

As she made her way toward the body of the house, she became aware of male voices. She picked her father's voice out easily enough. But the other, a rich baritone, slid a shiver down her spine. Probably a construction worker, she rationalized to assuage the sudden apprehension gripping her.

She found Mikey in the expansive living space sitting on a leather couch in front of a flat-screen plasma television watching his favorite cartoon. The great room, with its twenty-foot-high ceiling and bank of windows overlooking a small lake, was elegantly styled in warm, earthy tones and expensive-looking furnishings. More of her mother's handiwork.

Viv stood beside Mikey. His gaze never strayed from the screen. His body didn't move. He gave no indication he knew she was there, which wasn't unusual when he was expending so much concentration on the television.

Ignoring the irritating cartoon, Viv laid a hand on Mikey's head and gently stroked his hair. "Morning, sweetie."

He grabbed her hand, gave a squeeze and then let go.

Their ritual. One that Doctor Mason had worked on with them. She'd learned the hard way not to try gaining Mikey's attention when he was engrossed in something. Didn't matter what it was; if anything disturbed him, he reacted. Sometimes with anger, sometimes with tears. But always loudly and nearly uncontrollably. Getting him to calm down took time and energy that at the moment she didn't want to spare. She left him to his program and sought out her father.

Though the kitchen had the same panoramic view of the lake and the high, exposed-beam ceiling and shiny hardwood floor as the rest of the house, the trappings in here were a departure from her mother's usual style. Rich red-toned granite countertops sporting bright red small appliances and shiny stainless steel major appliances called for attention. But it was the tall, dark-haired man standing beside the island and towering over her father who drew her gaze as she stopped short.

Probing, coffee-colored eyes assessed her from beneath lashes most women would give their eyeteeth for. A roman nose and blunt jaw completed the face that could rival Michelangelo's *David*. The stranger was dressed in a black custom-tailored suit, if she wasn't mistaken, with a crisp white dress shirt and a thin black tie. Ray Ban sunglasses hung from the breast pocket of his suit jacket.

He had broad shoulders and a trim waist. His black slacks hung just right over his polished black dress shoes. He looked like he'd stepped out of an advertisement from the pages of a *GQ* magazine or was the poster boy for the federal government. Like Will Smith and Tommy Lee Jones in *Men in Black*. The two agents who'd taken her for a ride last night had nothing on this guy.

Viv narrowed her gaze as suspicion and wariness infiltrated her mind. She didn't trust anyone right now. "Dad, you called the feds? After what they did?"

"What? Oh, no, no. Not to worry, my girl.

You'll be in good hands. Carlucci's no longer with the government."

Carlucci arched a raven-colored eyebrow ever so slightly. He held out his hand. "Anthony Carlucci. I'm with Trent Associates. Your father has apprised us of the situation."

Her gaze flickered to his outstretched hand then back to his face. "The situation being that I found my husband murdered and then fake FBI agents drove me to a secluded place where they were going to do…who knew what?"

"Exactly," her father said. "Trent Associates specializes in personal security. Mr. Carlucci has intimate knowledge of Washington politics and law enforcement."

"Really." She couldn't keep her doubts out of her tone. Just how was this going to play out?

Her gaze slid to her father. His craggy face gave away nothing. Even at nearly seventy, his white hair was thick and his body muscled from years of working alongside his men in the mines. "Why did you do this?"

"I can't stay with you any longer without telling your mother what is going on. You'll be safer if you turn yourself in. And it's only a matter of time before your whereabouts are discovered."

Either by the police or Steven's killer. A shiver of dread rippled over her.

Carlucci inclined his head in agreement. "Your father has hired me to help you navigate through the mire of red tape associated with the investigation of your husband's death."

Not liking the undertone of accusation in his voice, she said, "I didn't kill my husband."

"You fled from the scene of a murder. That doesn't look good," he shot back. "The D.C. police and the FBI will have questions."

"Didn't you hear me?" She stared at him incredulously. "Two men claiming to be from the FBI picked Mikey and me up from the house. They drove us to a secluded part of town and we barely got away."

He was quiet for a moment. "I checked into the story you told your father. Officer Peal tells a different version."

Shock siphoned the oxygen from her brain. She gripped the counter for support. "Excuse me? What does he say?"

"He claims to have put you in a cruiser. Then while he checked with his men, you and your son took off."

This was unbelievable. "That's not true. He talked to those men who took us. They even had badges that looked real." She grabbed for her bag sitting on the counter and dug out a piece of paper. She held it out to Carlucci. "I wrote down the license plate number of the SUV. Run the plates. You'll see I'm telling the truth."

His skeptical expression unnerved her. He tucked the paper into his jacket pocket.

Desperately, she turned to her father. "You believe me, don't you?"

There was the briefest hesitation before her father answered, "Of course. That's why I called Trent. He sent Carlucci."

"To do what?" she nearly shouted. "Take us in, all neat and tidy like a pretty package?"

Carlucci's eyebrows dipped. "As I've already explained, I'm here to protect you and make sure you're treated fairly."

A knot the size of a fist lodged in her chest. They all suspected her of killing Steven and making up the agents. "Shouldn't I have a lawyer, not a…" She waved a hand, not sure what to call him.

"A bodyguard," her father finished for her.

"Right. A bodyguard. Unbelievable."

"I am in fact a lawyer as well as…a bodyguard."

"That makes me feel so much better." *Not.*

Distrust and doubt flickered in Carlucci's eyes. She didn't like the way this man stared at her as if seeking her secrets so he could determine her guilt or innocence. Viv didn't care what the man thought as long as he protected her son.

Her gaze snagged on a file folder sitting on the island next to her carryall bag. Her name was on the label. She didn't like that this stranger had a dossier on her.

"Do you know any reason why someone wanted your husband dead?" Carlucci asked.

"Not off the top of my head. He was a politician. Politicians tend to have enemies. You'd need to speak to his secretary."

The sound of shuffling feet dragged Viv's attention to Mikey. He stopped beside her, his bear clenched in his hand. Love filled her heart and eased some of the tension in her shoulders. "Hi, sweetie," she said, moving toward him.

"Hungry."

Slipping her arm around him, she was in the process of squatting to look in his eyes when Carlucci shouted, "Sniper!"

Before she could even shift her gaze to her bodyguard, she was tackled by a hard driving body, taking both her and Mikey to the ground. She cried out as the kitchen window exploded. Something passed within inches of her head to embed itself in the island cabinet.

Another bullet slammed into the floor beside Mikey.

Shock dulled the pain of impact. She grappled to make sense of what was happening. Someone was shooting at them.

"Behind the counter, now!" her new bodyguard commanded as he pushed at her and Mikey. "Move!"

Reality slammed into her brain as she scrambled to the other side of the island. She gripped Mikey close, though he squirmed to be set free. Anthony pressed his back to the cabinet and pulled a gun from a shoulder holster hidden beneath his jacket. He checked the clip.

"Mr. LeMar?" Carlucci shouted.

"I'm fine," her father replied from somewhere on the other side of the island. "Viv, Mikey?"

"They're unhurt." Carlucci turned to stare at her as if making sure his words were true.

Viv blinked at him in horror. "Just what kind of bodyguard are you? You led them right to us."

* * *

With his back pressed against the cupboard, Anthony yanked his gaze from the stunning woman beside him. He chanced a look around the kitchen island out the now nonexistent window toward where the glare of sunlight had bounced off what could only have been a rifle scope.

Granite exploded on the island's surface. Pieces of stone stung Anthony's face. He drew back. The muzzle flash put the shooter on a ridge to the left of center roughly four hundred meters away on the other side of the lake. A lone shooter?

"I can't believe this. From one nightmare to another," Vivian Grant groused beside him. "You're sure not worth whatever my father is paying you."

Anthony glared at the blonde. The minute he'd seen her photo, he'd known she'd be trouble. Too pretty, too smart and too spoiled.

Her already pale complexion had gone pasty and her sky-blue eyes held a mixture of dazed shock and righteous anger. But clearly Miss Idaho Potato wasn't the type to mash under pressure. Good for her. All that polished exterior better not be just for show. He needed her to keep her head if they were to get out of here alive.

"Look, lady, no one followed me here. I didn't even know I was going anywhere until an hour before I boarded a plane. And I came from Boston, not D.C." So it was more likely she'd been followed, but pointing that out right now wouldn't get them out of the situation. "Mr. LeMar, we need wheels."

"The garage," Ben LeMar said as he crawled on his belly, military-fashion, into view from around the other end of the island. He gestured with his head. "This way."

Anthony positioned himself between the bank of windows and Vivian and the child. He nudged them toward the now open doorway. The stove took a hit; the distinct ping of metal hitting metal filled the air.

Vivian duck walked forward and coaxed her son to move. "Come on, Mikey. Follow grandpa."

The kid tried to stand, but his mother pulled him back down. "No, like this, honey." She demonstrated by crawling on hands and knees. The kid didn't budge.

Placing a hand on the kid's back, Anthony urged the child into action. Mikey reared away with a squawk.

"Don't touch him," Viv shouted as she made a grab for her son but missed. He scrambled out of reach and stood next to the stove.

"I wasn't going to hurt him," Anthony snapped, yanking the child back down just as a bullet whizzed past and smacked with a thud into the wall behind the stove.

What was up with the kid? He was old enough to understand they needed to keep low and get out of the line of fire. Exasperated with them both, he growled to Mrs. Grant, "Get to the garage. I'll bring your son."

"My bag!" In a swift move, she grabbed the black bag from the counter. Another bullet barely missed her. She cried out and dove out of the way.

Grinding his teeth in frustration, Anthony charged forward in a crouch with the squirming kid tucked under his good arm and hustled his mother out the door with the other arm. The kid swatted at him, his small hands barely registering against his forearms, while making high-pitched noises that could wake the dead. As soon as they were clear and in the safety of the garage, Vivian rushed to take her son from Anthony's grasp.

LeMar shoved a set of keys at Anthony, his face a mask of concern and anger. "Take the Range Rover. The steel's reinforced. There's a map inside. Once you get them to safety, call me."

Fear clouded Vivian's blue gaze. "What about you, Dad?"

LeMar chucked his daughter under the chin. "No problem. I'll take the Humvee and go out the back way of the subdivision. If we separate, they won't know which vehicle to follow."

The plan had merit. Anthony needed to get his clients out of there before their would-be assassin decided on a more up close and personal approach.

"Get in," he ordered, opening the rear door of the backed-in Range Rover.

"Get in," Mikey mimicked in a voice eerily like Anthony's.

Viv slid onto the backseat and pulled Mikey onto her lap.

Anthony opened the driver's door. LeMar stopped him with a hand on his shoulder. "You take care of them."

Anthony's gut twisted. His shoulder throbbed, reminding him of the last time he'd been charged with someone's safety. He hated being in this position. What had he been thinking when he'd agreed to take this job?

"I will, sir." He climbed into the front seat and started the engine. "Stay down and out of sight," he cautioned the pair in the backseat.

Without a word, Viv sank to the floor of the backseat.

Mikey was still making his high-pitched wails. Viv wrapped her arms around him and gently rocked. Anthony could feel the kid's agitation with solid kicks against the leather backrest of the driver's seat. The garage door rumbled open too slowly. Anthony's fingers flexed on the steering wheel. He revved the engine. The second the door was high enough, LeMar, in the bright yellow Humvee, roared out of the garage, down the short drive and took a sharp left.

Anthony threw the dark green Range Rover into gear and sped out of the garage, turning right. He gunned the motor and zipped toward the subdivision's front entrance. Nerves stretched tight, he kept a sharp eye out.

Five minutes later he hit the highway and drove the Rover to the limit, dicing through the mid-morning traffic and around curves like a pro racer. Or more like he was driving a go-cart from his youth.

When he was sure they were far enough away and not being followed, he said, "You can sit up now."

Vivian slowly rose. "I think I'm going to be sick."

In the rearview mirror's reflection she did look a bit green. "That would be very unfortunate."

Her gaze collided with his. The beautiful ice-blue eyes could freeze a man to the core or melt him to a puddle.

"You think?" her voice dripped with sarcasm.

Anthony jerked his attention back to the road. He had no intention of freezing or melting. Staying detached and unemotionally involved with his client could be the difference between life and death. But it hadn't made a difference for the Kashmir delegate. The painful thought settled in his stomach like a rock.

Behind him, Mikey had quieted down. No more jabs to Anthony's kidneys through the back of his seat. "He okay?" he asked, keeping his gaze on the road.

"Yes. Car rides usually calm him."

"Can you direct us to the airport?"

"Where are we going?"

"Back to D.C."

"It's not safe there."

He heard the thread of fear in her tone. "You'll have to trust me. You'll be safer in the custody of real federal agents than out in the open."

"Yeah, right," she muttered.

"The sooner we're on a plane heading east the better."

"Well…"

The hesitation in her voice pricked his alarm. "Well?"

"It's just…"

He sought her gaze through the mirror, again. "Just what?"

Her top teeth tugged at her bottom lip. "I don't know how long Mikey will stay calm. He usually has a very set schedule. He tolerated the plane ride here because he slept for most of it. But…"

"We'll deal with any tantrums." Boy, the kid had her wrapped around his finger. "You're the parent. He'll have to do as you say."

She sighed. "If it were only that simple."

"Why isn't it?"

"How much do you know about me? About us?" she asked, her eyes piercing him through the mirror's reflection.

He mentally went over the thin dossier he'd read on the plane from Boston, that was still on the counter back at the house they'd just fled. "Your husband was the sitting junior senator for the state of Idaho. He had just declared his intent to run for the presidency. You've been married for nearly twelve years and you have one son, Michael Steven Grant."

He didn't mention other details, such as her husband's string of affairs dating back to when he was a councilman for the city of Boise and the numerous beauty pageant wins of the stunning Vivian Leigh LeMar Grant.

"Well, Steven was careful to keep much of our lives private. Mikey has PDD/NOS."

"Which is…?"

"Pervasive Developmental Disorder, Not Otherwise Specified. A fancy way of saying he has autism with characteristics that can't be easily checked off on some form to determine a precise diagnosis."

Okay. Explained the kid's behavior. Though Anthony had no practical experience with the disorder, the media was filled with stories of children with autism.

His earlier assessment of Viv and Mikey's relationship shifted. She had a hard road to travel with her son. A seed of respect planted itself in his mind. Not only had she not flown into hysterics while bullets were flying, she'd focused on her son, on calming him, protecting him. Like a good mother.

Could she have killed her husband to protect her son? But if she had, then who was using her as target practice? Her accomplice?

"If you didn't kill your husband and don't know who did, then why would someone want you dead?" he asked.

Silence met his question. He needed answers before he went any further. Up ahead he saw a fast-food joint. He turned into the lot and drove around to the back, out of sight of the road. After turning off the engine, he shifted on the seat so he could face Viv. "I repeat, why does someone want you dead?"

She shrugged, her gaze downcast. "My husband was just murdered. What do you want me to say?"

"I need you to answer the question."

After another beat of silence, he reached out and took her fisted hand out of her lap. Her hand was cold and soft and fit easily within his palm. "Look, the sooner you're straight with me, the sooner we can figure out the best plan of action. For the duration of our time together, I'm your bodyguard and your lawyer. Anything you tell me is confidential."

Her ice-blue eyes flashed with anger as she yanked her hand out of his. "You think I had something to do with Steven's murder."

"I think you're mixed up in something dangerous that resulted in your husband's death. But I can't help you unless you tell me the truth."

She studied him, her expression one of distrust and something else. Hope or fear, he wasn't sure. Then her gaze slid to her son. The kid stared straight ahead with big round, midnight-blue eyes. He worried his left index finger.

Finally, Viv leaned forward and in a low voice said, "Mikey witnessed his father's murder. That's why someone wants us dead."

Surprise kicked him in the chest. He hadn't expected that. "Tell me what happened."

As she explained the events from that night, Anthony couldn't help wondering if the plausible story was true. There was something off about the way she talked about her deceased husband, devoid of emotion, no grief, nothing. "So let me get this straight, Mikey was under the desk?"

"Yes. You'd have to see the desk. It's massive and one of Mikey's favorite places to hide." Viv glanced toward the burger place. "Since we're here, I'd like to use the facilities."

Anthony faced forward. There was no one lurking about in the back parking lot and they were hidden from the main road. The restrooms inside the restaurant were visible through the glass windows. "Of course. You have five minutes."

He opened the door and climbed out. The air smelled of hamburgers and grease, making him aware he needed food. He started around the car but Vivian was already standing beside the vehicle trying to coax Mikey out.

"Need help?"

"No," she huffed. "Mikey, come on."

The kid finally slid out and docilely followed his mother inside the restaurant to the restroom. A big shift in behavior from the fit the kid had thrown when he'd picked him up and carried him out of the house.

Anthony leaned against the side of the Range Rover and pulled the paper with the license plate number from his pocket. He wasn't buying Viv's story. But it wouldn't hurt to have the numbers run and see what turned up. He reached for his cell. Rather than using his contacts in D.C., he called Trent Associates and gave the information to Simone. She put him on hold.

Man, this job wasn't as easy as he'd been led to believe. The mountains rising in the distance were as intractable as Miss Cornflower with her cool good looks and barely concealed distrust.

The assignment had sounded simple enough. Bring Vivian Grant to the feds and act as her counsel—good thing he'd maintained a license to practice law in D.C., not that he'd ever intended to use it before—during the murder investigation of her husband.

Simple? Yeah, right. Until someone started shooting at them.

Because her autistic son might be a witness? Or because Vivian Grant was somehow involved in her husband's demise?

THREE

Wendell Brooks rapped on his boss's door. Anxiety churned in his gut. The news he'd just received wasn't good.

"Enter!"

Bracing himself, he opened the door, entered the office and carefully closed the door behind him. "Sir. We've encountered a snag I think you should be aware of."

His boss jerked his attention from the documents on the desk to spear Wendell with a hard glare. "Snag?"

"In the Grant problem," Wendell clarified and rushed into an explanation, likening delivering bad news to ripping off a sticky bandage. Best to get it over with as quickly as possible. "Mrs. Grant and her son got away."

"What?"

Wendell winced. "Our shooter missed. But we're still tracking the woman and the boy. It's just getting a bit more complicated.

There's another player involved. I had Mr. LeMar's phone records pulled. Right after his daughter called his cell on Friday night, Mr. LeMar called a Boston-based company, Trent Associates. They specialize in personal security. We think Mrs. Grant and her son have a bodyguard."

The crack of a palm hitting wood echoed in the expansive office, making Wendell jump.

"Then deal with this bodyguard as well. What am I paying you for? Get it done. We can't afford any more mess-ups."

"Yes, sir," Wendell said and bolted from the room. There'd been no mistaking the implied threat in his boss's tone. If the Grant problem wasn't taken care of soon, Wendell would become the next problem that needed taking care of.

Wendell placed his hand over his heart and felt the small recording device hidden inside the breast pocket of his suit jacket, taking comfort in his life insurance.

Inside the dingy fast-food joint's bathroom, Viv braced her hands on either side of the sink and hung her head. Mikey yanked on the door handle, wanting out. How had her life come to this?

The answer lay trapped in her lungs like

smoke, corroding her inside. She exhaled a breath to push out the poisonous reality. She had no one to blame for her situation but herself. It didn't matter that she'd grown up fearing her mother's punishments if she hadn't done as she'd been told. By the time she was eighteen, she should have developed enough spine to stand up to her mother's manipulations and intimidations. But she hadn't. Her spirit had been broken for too many years and she'd been too afraid of the consequences of defying her mother.

So when her father had presented her with a way out from under her mother's thumb, Viv had taken it. Marrying the suave and dashing Steven Grant had seemed like a godsend. Which turned into another nightmare she had to survive.

The only bright spot was Mikey.

Regardless of her son's challenges, she knew deep in her soul that God had a plan. A plan for Mikey. A plan for her. She could never forget that, no matter how horrible her circumstances. God meant for her to protect Mikey. She would do anything for her son.

Even put their lives in the hands of a stranger.

A man who didn't believe her when she

said she didn't kill her husband. Suspicion was clear in his warm brown eyes.

Anger stirred. He didn't know her. Didn't know the life she'd had to live or the heartache she suffered. How dare he suspect her without any evidence?

She let out a short laugh. No doubt everyone would suspect her, the wife. Didn't they always?

She turned on the faucet. The sound of running water drew Mikey's attention to the sink, as she knew it would. He plunged his hands beneath the cool stream. The tactile sensation would keep him momentarily distracted.

Above Mikey's head, she stared at her reflection in the hazy mirror under the harsh fluorescent light. Her features were symmetrically proportionate, her eyes a unique shade of blue that always drew compliments, her skin flawless, her hair natural and thick. Everything most women wanted.

She despised the outside package of the woman staring back at her. Her beauty had cost her so much. If only she'd looked more like her father than her mother, then maybe she would have had a normal childhood, a normal marriage.

But lamenting what she had no control over didn't accomplish anything other than to stir up discontent and resentment. She would not let either take hold in her soul.

No matter how easy doing so would be.

She moistened a paper towel and blotted her face and neck, mentally preparing herself for what was to come. She needed her "bodyguard" for protection, not only from their assailant, but also from the law.

Could she trust this man with her and her son's lives?

Her lips twisted with a scoff. She didn't know much about her bodyguard, other than he was nice to look at. Not enough of a reason to place her life in his hands.

Her father must trust him to have hired him to protect them. Was that enough of a reason for Viv too?

For now, she decided, it was. Because really, what choice did she have?

She sighed. It seemed life was always out of her control. Only her faith kept her sane.

Squaring her shoulders, she schooled her features. She'd do what needed to be done, for Mikey's sake. His safety and well-being were her top priority.

With that thought firmly ingrained in her mind, she turned off the faucet and opened the bathroom door. Like a rocket, Mikey ran out of the small bathroom, down the short hall and through the outer door before she could even think of trying to catch him. She hurried after him. She blinked when the sunlight hit her.

As she approached the Range Rover, her breath stalled. Her heart ratcheted up. Mikey and the bodyguard were nowhere in sight. Fear threw the switch on panic. She turned and ran toward the front of the burger joint, frantically searching for her son.

Vivian skidded to a halt. Inside the fast-food restaurant, Mikey and Carlucci were standing in line to order. Relief spiraled through her, making her legs wobbly. She entered the restaurant but stayed near the door. Carlucci ordered, paid, and a few moments later the clerk handed him a bag. Mikey grew agitated. His hands started to flap.

Quickly, Carlucci dug into the bag and produced a small box of French fries. Mikey stilled and listened as Anthony said something before handing over the box. Mikey slowly walked beside Anthony, allowing the man to put his arm around his thin shoulders as he chomped on the little potato sticks.

She blinked back sudden tears as something so unexpected she wasn't sure the sensation had a name gripped her. Tenderness? But so much more than that. And she couldn't decipher whether the feeling was directed at her son or the man paying attention to him. Or both?

Anthony met her gaze. The kindness she saw in the near-black irises made her pulse jump. Good-looking *and* kind? A lethal combination.

"Hope you don't mind, but he wanted French fries." Anthony regarded her with a hint of uncertainty as they approached her.

"No, that's…that's fine." Her heartbeat finally resumed its normal cadence. Her son was safe. That was all that mattered.

"You might want to grab a bite to eat now rather than at the airport," Carlucci said.

She hesitated. She was hungry; she hadn't had time to eat before the bullets started flying. Only problem was her bag with her wallet was still in the Rover. "I can wait."

Her stomach growled, refuting her words. Heat crept up her neck.

He frowned and reached inside his suit jacket, withdrawing a billfold. He took out a twenty and offered it to her. "Just get something. Be quick about it."

She snatched the twenty. "Do you want anything?"

He held up the bag in his hand. "I'm covered." His gaze shot to Mikey who continued to munch on fries. "Wasn't sure what else he'd eat."

Grateful for his thoughtfulness, she said, "I'll get him some chicken nuggets."

When she had her and Mikey's food in hand, they returned to the Range Rover. Once they were on the road headed toward the airport, she settled beside Mikey to eat her chicken sandwich. Though she barely tasted her food, she knew eating had been a good decision. She felt calmer and more alert.

The sudden acceleration of the Rover revved through Viv's blood. She grabbed the overhead handle with her right hand and placed her left arm across Mikey's body. Anthony maneuvered the vehicle through traffic, cutting in and out between cars. Her stomach rolled. Dread throbbed at her temples.

Beside her Mikey's hands began to flap. "No, no," he wailed.

"What's wrong?" she shouted over Mikey's cries.

"We've got a tail," he said, his face a study in concentration as he drove, angling the Rover across two lanes. Horns honked in protest.

Viv turned to look through the back tinted window. It wasn't hard to pick out the car chasing them. A gold sedan made the same risky move across the traffic, keeping pace. "How'd they find us?"

"Don't know. Hang on," Anthony shouted.

Please don't let us crash, she silently prayed.

The Rover shot down the next exit and squealed around the corner, then bounced over the curb, across the sidewalk and into the parking lot of a shopping center. She felt like she'd stepped into some action flick. Surreal. Expertly, Anthony slid the Rover into a parking place between two trucks and threw the gear into park.

Shutting off the engine, he said, "Come on. We've got to move."

Adrenaline spiked. Viv unbuckled and then undid Mikey. Not taking the time to coax, she pulled Mikey out by the arm. He protested with a loud wail and tried to pull away. She held on tight. Then Anthony appeared beside her, lifting Mikey into the cradle of his arms while Mikey squirmed, but he was no match for their bodyguard's strength. For which she was grateful.

"Go, go," Anthony urged. "Inside the mall."

They ran through the parking lot. People stared. Something Viv had grown used to. Mikey looked normal, like any other kid his age, but his behavior drew gawkers. Viv was sure someone would call the cops. Who wouldn't when they saw a man running with a child who was struggling to be set free? But what choice did they have? Viv stayed on Anthony's heels as they entered the center.

"We have to find another exit," Anthony said as he slowed to a fast walk.

"There." Viv pointed toward the coffee shop on their right. She could see an outside door on the opposite side of the mall from where they entered.

Anthony headed in that direction. Viv caught one of Mikey's hands.

"Down," Mikey said. "Want down."

"I know. Just a few more minutes," she replied as she kept pace.

Once they entered the coffee shop and were seated in a corner booth near the exit, Anthony set Mikey on his feet but kept a firm hand on his shoulder, preventing him from moving away. Viv's heart squeezed tight. Steven had rarely touched their son.

"We've got to find a way out of here," Anthony stated, his watchful gaze locked on the entrance.

"Shouldn't we call the police?"

His eyes shifted toward her, his expression

hardened. "We could. Is that what you want to do?"

Turmoil churned in Viv's stomach. She wasn't sure what she wanted or what to think. Twice now they'd been found. The next time they might not escape. She couldn't help but wonder if Anthony had somehow given them away. But he seemed capable. He certainly knew how to drive a car at breakneck speeds. And she'd already decided to try trusting him. After all, her father was thorough. He wouldn't have hired an incompetent protection agency.

She thought about how easily Officer Peal released her and Mikey to the custody of the two men who'd claimed to be agents. Would the Boise police be as easily fooled if another set of fake agents arrived?

At the moment Anthony was the only buffer they had. She shook her head. "No."

An unidentifiable emotion crossed his features before he nodded. "Good. I'll call Trent and see how quickly someone can come get us."

Viv glanced out the exit door into the parking lot. An older woman was loading several shopping bags into the trunk of her big Cadillac. The woman looked like a grandmother.

"I have a better idea." Taking Mikey by the hand, she pushed past Anthony and out the door.

"Hey, wait!" he exclaimed.

She kept walking, forcing him to follow. Viv made a beeline for the woman and car. "Excuse me, I'm hoping maybe you can help us."

Surprise widened the woman's gray eyes. Wrinkles creased her face. She smiled at Mikey and then glanced at Anthony with curiosity. "Sure, if I can."

Counting on the friendliness of most people in Idaho, Viv said, "Our car won't work and we really need to get to the airport. We have a plane to catch. Would you, by any chance, be willing to give us a lift? We could pay you."

"Oh, goodness." The woman bit her lip, her suddenly wary gaze darting between the three of them.

Vivian offered her as much of the truth as she could. "My son is autistic. All this upheaval is difficult for him. I just need to get him home," Viv said and blinked back the unexpected tears burning her eyes.

Sympathy softened the older woman's gaze. "Oh, my. My friend Gertrude from Bible study has an autistic grandson. Traveling with him is never easy. I suppose I could drop you off. The airport is only about fifteen minutes from here. It's not too far out of my way."

Relief washed over Viv. She took the woman's hand between her own. "God bless you. Thank you so much, Mrs...?"

"Dear me, where are my manners? Edna Wilson." She gestured to the gold Cadillac. "Please, climb in."

Anthony opened the back door for Viv. Approval filled his dark eyes when she glanced at him. For some odd reason his appreciation warmed her.

"Come on, baby," she prodded Mikey, urging him to climb in. Anthony took shotgun with Mrs. Wilson at the wheel.

"Don't like here," Mikey groused and squirmed to be released from the seat belt. "Home."

"I know, honey." Viv wanted home, too. Only she didn't know where home was now. Certainly not at the Washington, D.C., house she'd shared with Steven. Not only was the place tainted by his death, but the years of silence and animosity that had become the norm between them would always haunt her, mocking her dream of a happy family.

With Steven gone Viv would have to find her and Mikey's place in the world. They were free to start over, anywhere. She could choose where to live, something she'd never been able to do for herself. And with the sale of the house and funds from the life insurance policy, she wouldn't have to worry about money for a while if she were conservative. She was kind of excited about what the future might hold for her and Mikey. She hadn't felt this way…in a very long time.

But first they had to get away from the people who wanted to kill them. And they had to clear her name.

After repeatedly refusing to accept any form of compensation for her trouble, Mrs. Wilson pulled to the curb of the departing passenger's de-loading zone of the Idaho airport terminal. "Have a safe trip."

Anthony glanced at Viv, grateful for her quick thinking. Viv waved goodbye to their Good Samaritan. As Mrs. Wilson drove away, Anthony propelled Viv and Mikey along through the bustling crowd of travelers to the bank of monitors showing the plane departures.

"There's a 6:30 p.m. flight to Dulles on United," Viv pointed out.

Anthony checked the time. Less than an hour. "Let's see if they have seats."

He steered them toward the ticket counter.

Mikey started shuffling back and forth as they waited in line. Viv whispered something in the kid's ear. Mikey nodded vigorously.

"I need to take him to the restroom," Viv said.

"Can he wait?"

She shook her head. "Not much longer."

Blowing out a frustrated breath, Anthony spotted the restrooms near a sports bar. He gestured in that direction. "Let's go."

With a tight smile, Viv nodded. With Mikey in tow they wove their way through the terminal.

To the left of the restrooms was a sports bar and grill. The sounds of the newscaster on the television hanging over the bar mingled with the clanging of dishware as people ate and drank. Anthony parked himself where the bar's railing met the wall to wait for Viv and Mikey.

His gaze roamed over the people coming and going, searching for some hint of danger. Minutes ticked by. Anthony checked his watch, his impatience growing. The plane would be boarding soon and their opportunity to purchase tickets would be gone. They were cutting it close. Too close.

From his peripheral view, he saw Viv and Mikey step out of the women's bathroom.

He pushed away from the wall just as the newscaster's voice snagged his attention. He thought he heard the name Senator Grant. Slowly, Anthony turned toward the TV screen.

A picture of Viv and Mikey flashed on the monitor. The newscaster, a Tom Selleck wannabe with a thick mustache said gravely, "Senator Steven Grant was found murdered in his Washington, D.C., home over the weekend. His wife, Vivian Grant, is the FBI's number one suspect. She disappeared shortly after the gruesome murder with her son. If you know the whereabouts of Vivian Grant or Michael Grant, please call the number you see at the bottom of the screen."

Shock sucker punched Anthony in the gut. Adrenaline surged in his veins. *Out, now.*

He spun around, captured Viv by the arm and started toward the exit at a fast clip. Aware of the multiple security cameras recording their presence, he said, "Keep your head down. We're getting out of here."

"Why? What happened?" she said in a breathless rush as she dragged Mikey along beside her.

"The FBI wants to charge you with murder."

FOUR

Heart pounding, Viv stepped out of the air-port terminal. She blinked at the stinging sun-light as she walked briskly to the far corner of the passenger vehicle loading area. Confusion thrummed through her. "What do you mean the FBI wants to charge me with murder?"

Anthony touched her elbow, urging her to turn away from the cars passing by. "Your pictures are plastered all over the TV news. You're the FBI's number one suspect in your husband's murder," Anthony replied.

She shuddered. "This can't be happening." She looked at Mikey, then cupped her hand over her mouth and whispered, "I didn't kill Steven."

"If you didn't, then someone is going to a lot of trouble to make it seem like you did," Anthony replied solemnly. "I had the license plate numbers run."

Eager for some proof she was telling the truth, she clutched his arm. "FBI, right?"

"Unregistered."

"Then that has to mean government." No one else could get away with driving an unregistered vehicle.

"Maybe. Maybe not."

Indignation flashed. "Are you kidding me?"

He still doubted her innocence even after the attempts on her life? For some reason that stung. Why would he believe the worst when he didn't know her?

He held up a hand. "Not my call. You two stay put for a moment."

With purposeful strides, he walked away and approached a man sitting on the bench in the designated smoking area. The two men talked a moment, then the man took off his hat and handed it to Anthony. In exchange, Anthony handed him some money.

He returned, handing her a battered cowboy hat. "Here, put this on."

"Is that really necessary?"

"Your blond hair stands out like a neon sign."

Pressing her lips together, she took the hat and tried not to grimace when she plopped it on her head.

"Pull it lower to shield your face," Anthony instructed.

She complied and caught a whiff of stale tobacco clinging to the hat's suede material. Though her eyes watered, she refused to complain.

"Obviously taking a commercial flight's not an option." Anthony removed his cell phone from his pocket. "I'll call Trent and see if he can arrange a private plane."

Viv touched his arm. "What about Mrs. Wilson? Once she sees the news, she'll call the police and they'll come here."

"Good point." With his cell phone at his ear, Anthony dialed and took a step away from her. "Carlucci here."

Hearing him discuss her and the situation so matter-of-factly to the other person on the line made Viv feel so vulnerable. Why was someone trying to destroy her?

Mikey tugged on the strap of her hobo bag, signaling he wanted a treat. She dug inside for a wrapped piece of hard candy. She handed it to him. He made quick work of the wrapper, putting the little piece of cellophane into her hand before popping the treat into his mouth.

"Sounds good," Anthony said and hung up. "Trent Associates has a corporate account with several rental-car agencies. We just need to get to one."

He hailed a taxi. Twenty minutes later Viv sat in the front passenger seat of a rented minivan; Anthony was behind the wheel with Mikey buckled in the back avidly watching a video on the built-in DVD player. The rental guy had even supplied them with a stack of movies which would keep her son entertained for a long time. One less thing to worry about.

Anthony handed her a road map as he drove toward the interstate highway.

"So what's the plan?" Viv asked.

"I'm taking you to Trent Associate's headquarters in Boston and we'll figure out what the next move is after that."

Dismay washed through Viv. Maybe she hadn't heard him correctly. "We're driving cross-country?"

"Yes. A private jet will attract attention. This will take us three days longer, but we're just another family taking a road trip."

A family. If only. Her heart ached. Anthony had no idea how badly she wished for a complete, happy family. She glanced over her shoulder at Mikey. He deserved a family. She sighed. Not going to happen. She was all he had. And if driving cross-country was the only way to ensure his safety then so be it. "This won't be easy."

A rueful expression played on Anthony's handsome face. "Very little in life is."

His statement piqued her curiosity. Was he jaded because of his work or had something happened to make him so cynical? The question lay on her tongue but she held back. The last thing she needed was to become emotionally involved in this man's life. He served a purpose. To get them to safety. Nothing more.

She spread out the map on her lap. "We take U.S. 20 to I-84 east to I-80 east and keep going until we hit Iowa. Then we'll merge onto I-280 east."

He nodded but didn't respond.

The distance on the map looked daunting. She sent up a silent prayer of protection. Hopefully, neither the bad guys nor the police would find them along the way. Viv stared out the window, watching the miles go by in a haze of anxiousness.

The silence became too much. She gave in to her curiosity about the man she'd entrusted her and her son's lives to. "How did you become a bodyguard?"

His hesitation sent a ribbon of uncertainty through her.

"I started out on the Boston police force," he said finally.

She tucked in her chin. "So wait. You're a bodyguard that was a government lawyer that was a Boston police officer? A little bit of an overachiever." But he still hadn't answered her question.

He shrugged. "I studied law at night after I joined the force. When I received my degree and gained my license, I applied for a government job."

"You didn't want to practice law?"

"No. Being an attorney was never my goal. I just needed the degree to do what I really wanted to do."

"Which was?" she asked.

"Work for the Treasury Department. Secret Service."

She raised her eyebrows. "And did you?"

"Yes."

Impressive. Guarding the President was a far cry from protecting the widow of a senator. "Why'd you leave the service?"

He slanted her a glance. "Does it matter?"

"To me it does."

"What difference will knowing make?"

She frowned. "Anthony, I have entrusted Mikey's well-being to very few people. I've taken a huge leap of faith in trusting you this far. I'm putting a lot of faith in your ability to keep Mikey safe."

His mouth pressed into a thin line. "Your faith probably won't help."

Apprehension bounced in her tummy. "That's not comforting. Care to tell me why?"

"Situations in which people like me are needed tend to be short on comfort."

"That's not what I meant."

He glanced at her. The world of hurt she saw in his eyes tugged at her heart. She wanted to ease the pain she saw there. Empathy prompted her to lift her hand to offer some sort of solace. His expression hardened as he shifted his gaze back to the road, making it clear he didn't want her compassion. Oddly hurt, she let her hand drop to her lap and folded her hands together. There was too much at stake to let raw emotions get in the way.

"The man I was protecting was assassinated on my watch."

Viv sucked in a stunned breath. Bad guys after them. The FBI suspecting her of murder. An unknown quantity of a bodyguard. And now this.

But she wouldn't jump to conclusions. Too many people had done so with her over the years. Even him, in thinking her capable of killing her husband. She wouldn't be guilty of the same thing with Anthony. She tried to follow the Golden Rule as best she could. "So did you make a mistake or was it just one of those unavoidable tragedies?"

Anthony gripped the steering wheel tighter. Feeling her gaze like a laser dot on his temple, he tried to decide how to answer her question. He settled on the line his superiors kept spouting. "When a bullet's got a name on it, there's nothing anyone can do once it leaves the barrel."

She made a strangled noise. "What does that even mean?"

"Good question," he said with a wry laugh. Her brains matched her beauty. "It means that even the best sometimes can't stop the inevitable, or so they say."

"You feel guilty for his death," she stated solemnly.

She didn't know the half of it. "Yeah, I do."

She was quiet for a moment. "Who died?"

He changed lanes, keeping his gaze alert for any signs of being followed. "A delegate from Kashmir who'd come to the U.S. seeking assistance in gaining peace between India and Pakistan."

"Those three countries have been at war since the forties," she said. "It's just so tragic."

"It is. India and Pakistan are in constant conflict over the territory of Kashmir. Each has nuclear capability and is prepared to use it if necessary."

"But war didn't break out when the dignitary was assassinated, right? I mean, we'd have heard something about it on the news."

"No, thankfully. The assassination wasn't related to the politics of the countries, but rather something to do with the personal life of the dignitary. Gambling."

She sat back. "Well, that's something at least."

"Yeah, at least."

But the shooting had killed his career and damaged his shoulder. Worse, it had eroded his confidence. Which this job was supposed to help rebuild. So far it hadn't.

"Tell me some more about your relationship with your husband. I want to be fully prepared when we face the authorities."

She gave a long-suffering sigh. "There's not much to tell. I married Steven right after my eighteenth birthday. I was in awe of this older man. Steven was kind and considerate. Dashing even. But it didn't take long to see the real him. Steven wasn't the best at interpersonal relationships. He did great in crowds and was a smooth politician, but…"

She shrugged. "Mikey came along four years later. I was so happy to have a child. Steven was happy to have a son. By the time Mikey was three I knew something was off. The autism diagnosis devastated Steven. My parents, or more specifically my mother, wanted me to put Mikey in a home. Steven agreed with her."

Anthony ached for Vivian, for the lack of support she apparently received. "That's harsh. Why did you stay married to him?"

Her expression made it clear she thought the question absurd. "I made a vow before God. Marriage is forever."

He liked her answer. In fact he found himself liking her a lot. "I agree marriage is forever. But he wanted to take your son away. Most people would have either bolted or capitulated."

"Yes, well, needless to say, I stayed and I didn't allow them to remove Mikey from me. I refused to bend under their pressure."

"That's very admirable. Shows a great strength of character."

She flashed a pleased and slightly embarrassed smile. "Thanks. That was the first time I'd ever stood up to my mother." Her mouth twisted in a cynical smirk. "She didn't like it much and still hasn't forgiven me."

"I take it you and your mother don't get along?"

"That would be an understatement. My mother is… Hmm, how best to describe her. The Wicked Witch of the West? *Mommie Dearest*."

"Ouch." So even her childhood hadn't been picture-perfect. Compassion welled up. "A bit tyrannical, huh?"

"Yes." She made a face. "So was Steven. I've spent my whole life under someone else's thumb."

Anthony cut her a sharp glance. Motive enough for murder? "Not anymore, now that your husband is dead."

Could that same strength of character he'd just admired be used to kill? Good thing he wouldn't have to make that judgment. He was just here to bring her to the authorities safely.

"True. And once this mess is resolved, Mikey and me will get to live our lives our way. Together."

Anthony glanced at Mikey in the rearview mirror. The boy sat rocking slightly, forward and back, his gaze out the front window. "You're very good with him."

"I don't have a choice." A soft smile teased her pretty mouth. "I love him. He's my son."

Anthony could appreciate her feelings even though he wasn't a parent and had no plans to be one any time soon. He knew his parents loved him and his siblings unconditionally. That was how it should be. Viv loved her son that way. Amazing considering her own mother sounded as far from unconditional as one could get.

"Don't you ever question why God allowed him to be born this way?"

"Not any more than I question why God allowed me to be born this way." She made a sweeping gesture toward herself. Then narrowing her gaze, she said, "Why would I blame God for something that could have been caused by any number of factors? All of which have more to do with the human condition than God. That would be as ludicrous as blaming God for Steven's murder."

His heart rate sped up. "But if you believe that God is all-powerful, all-knowing, couldn't He prevent these things?"

"You sound just like Steven." She turned away to stare out the window. "Believe me, Steven tried to find the reason behind Mikey's disorder. Something, someone to blame. It's convenient and easy to blame God. Humans do it all the time."

Anthony's throat tightened. Her words pierced his soul like arrows. He didn't want to look at why her words were creating so much havoc inside of him. He flexed his fingers and readjusted his grip on the steering wheel.

"There just isn't any definitive explanation for Mikey's condition. It could have been our genetics. It could have been some environmental element I came in contact with during pregnancy, or vaccines, food allergies…the list of possible reasons is endless."

The frustration in her voice ripped into him. Compassion welled. He didn't know what to say, how to comfort her.

"As for Steven's death…good ol' mankind." She shook her head. "So no, I don't blame God. I cling to Him."

I cling to Him. The words reverberated inside Anthony's head as the miles whizzed by.

There definitely was more to the beauty queen than met the eye. Smart, compassionate and a good parent to boot. And if her story about fighting off the fake FBI agents was true, she hid an admirable fierceness within her polished exterior.

All of which made her an intriguing woman. He was finding himself not only attracted to her, but liking her. If the situation were different…

But it wasn't. She was his protectee. Attraction, liking, none of those soft emotions had any place in the equation.

He needed to concentrate on the one question he couldn't let go of. Was she involved in her husband's murder?

It was nearly midnight by the time Anthony pulled the minivan into the parking lot of a convenience store. Viv stirred as the engine quieted. She'd fallen asleep somewhere in Utah. She'd looked so vulnerable and sweet leaned against the door, using his suit coat as a pillow.

Viv straightened and looked around. "Where are we?"

"On the outskirts of Cheyenne, Wyoming. I need to grab a few things before we stop for the night." He needed to rest, but they needed to do something about disguising Viv and Mikey.

She nodded and pulled the awful hat down lower. After her initial protest she'd kept the thing on her head for the past ten hours to keep her identity hidden from passing motorists. She was a trouper and that went a long way in his book.

Quietly, he left the van, locking the doors with the electronic key before entering the store. Buying the necessary supplies didn't take long and he hustled back to the van. Easily finding the motel the store clerk suggested, Anthony checked them into connecting rooms on the second floor. Vivian had become more fully awake while he was in the motel's small office. He handed her a card key.

He parked in front of the staircase, noting the other vehicles in the parking lot—a sedan, another minivan, two pick-up trucks and a big rig taking up the back half of the lot. Anthony carried a sleeping Mikey to the room while his mom carried their few belongings and the bag from the store. Viv used the key card to open the door and quickly turned down one of the double beds.

He gently laid Mikey down. Viv immediately went to work on removing his shoes. For a moment Anthony watched the loving way she so carefully untied each shoe and slipped them from the sleeping boy. Her love was so evident and constant.

Inexplicably, his throat tightened. He hadn't given much thought to having a family of his own. Sure, he'd wanted to marry Becca, but she'd had her career and he'd had his. Having kids hadn't been part of their conversations. Kids had been something to think about far into the future. A future that no longer existed.

Pushing away the unwanted memory of his former fiancée, Anthony forced himself to turn away from the appealing mother and son moment and focused on the here and now. He moved to open the two connecting doors. "I'll be right back."

Going out the door in his room, he hurried down to the parking lot. Not wanting to advertise their whereabouts, he hid the van behind a metal garage bin, just in case anyone traced them to the rental agency.

When he returned to the hotel rooms, Viv sat at the foot of one of the double beds with the bag from the grocery store in her lap.

"Sunglasses? Ball caps?" she asked, taking out the three pairs of shades he'd bought. Two adult-size, one child-size. The baseball caps had the Boise State University Broncos' logo on the front.

"There are security cameras everywhere. There's no way to avoid them, but if we wear the sunglasses and caps, and keep our heads tilted down, facial recognition won't have enough markers to make a match."

She pulled more items from the bag.

"Hair dye? Scissors?"

"We need to change your look. Your hair is too identifiable."

She held up the box of hair coloring he'd purchased and gave him a lopsided smile that made him forget his name. "I've always wondered what it would be like to be a brunette. I was named after Vivien Leigh from *Gone with the Wind*. Which always seemed odd to me since I look nothing like her."

She gave a delicate shrug. "But my mom's obsessed with the movie. I think she secretly wanted to be Scarlett O'Hara. She tried to talk daddy into naming me Scarlett. The only reason he agreed to Vivian Leigh is because his great-grandmother was named Vivian. Though Mom had a fit when she realized he'd filled out my birth certificate and spelled *Vivian* with an *A* like his grandmother's name, rather than *Vivien* with an *E* like the actress." A flush of color rose up her neck. "I'm sorry I'm babbling. Nerves, I guess."

Respect for how well she was taking the situation constricted his chest. "You're doing fine."

He pulled her to her feet; her hand, delicate

and yet solid at the same time, fit neatly within his.

"Can we use the bathroom in your room so we don't wake Mikey?"

"Absolutely." He led her back to his room. Taking the grocery bag from her he set it aside. "We'll change Mikey's hair color in the morning."

Meeting his gaze, she said, "It'll be challenging."

"I know." If he'd learned anything in the past day, it was that Vivian was a good mother and Mikey was a handful. Admiration for her dug in deep.

With a nod, she moved into the bathroom. "The directions say to use it on dry hair." She paused and slowly turned toward him with a look of concern. "These are the only clothes I have. I'd rather not ruin them."

"I figured you'd need something else to wear." He reached into the grocery bag and pulled out the two tourist T-shirts he'd bought. "This will have to do for now. They only had extra large." He tossed her a shirt. "In the morning we can stop and buy a change of clothes for all of us."

She caught the shirt. "I'll need help."

"That's what I'm here for."

"Yeah? Hair Color 101…after ballistics and before hand-to-hand training?"

Liking her humor, he laughed. "Yeah, something like that."

He slipped out of his jacket, removed his shoulder holster, draping them over the arm of a chair and then began unbuttoning his white dress shirt.

Vivian stood frozen in the doorway of the bathroom, staring.

He raised his eyebrows at her.

She did an abrupt about-face and shut the door, but not before Anthony glimpsed the blush working its way up her delicate neck.

So Miss Dew Berry Princess wasn't immune to the attraction he'd been fighting since the moment he'd laid eyes on her. Interesting. And probably not the best time to catch on to that fact considering he had no business noticing.

He made quick work of changing into the second T-shirt before knocking lightly on the bathroom door. "You decent?"

The door opened. Viv had exchanged her soft sweater and slacks for the too-large shirt, which hung past her knees. Anthony's gaze swept down her slender, well-shaped calves to her pink-polished toes. He struggled to swallow.

She cleared her throat for obviously different reasons, jerking his attention to her face. He grinned. He was a guy after all. He couldn't help looking. She blushed again. The urge to pull her into his arms caught him by surprise.

"Could you go next door and get some more towels?" she asked, her voice sounding a bit strangled.

Glad for the momentary reprieve from the searing attraction, he nodded. "Be right back."

He turned on his heel and went after the towels.

Get a grip, Carlucci. She's off-limits. You can not get involved with a protectee.

Vivian closed the door behind Anthony and leaned back against the wood, trying to regain her composure. Her heart galloped in her chest. Her cheeks still burned. What was happening? She'd been stared at with male appreciation her whole life. She'd thought she'd become immune to stares that normally made her feel like some museum piece to be studied and appraised.

But Anthony didn't make her feel that way. He made her feel feminine and pretty. She'd wanted to preen, of all things. And that surprised her. Stunned her, really.

When was the last time she'd felt that way? Long enough ago that she couldn't remember.

After her marriage, she'd been the proper wife and never purposefully set out to draw another man's attention. She'd dressed conservatively and avoided compromising situations.

But something about Carlucci made her feel brazen. She'd wanted to flirt, to see if Anthony felt the same sort of attraction that sizzled in her veins. She'd wanted... She released a pent-up breath, straightened her shoulders and pushed away from the door.

It didn't matter what she wanted.

Her wants didn't matter. Developing feelings for her bodyguard that couldn't go anywhere wasn't going to help them.

What she needed to do was stay the course, to do what had to be done to keep her and Mikey safe. To do that, she needed to change her looks so no one would recognize her as Senator Grant's widow.

Normally she paid one hundred and fifty dollars for haircuts. Her highlights added another hundred to the tab, not to mention the tip. But this wasn't La Bella Salon in trendy Georgetown. She had a cheap pair of scissors and not much light.

Her stylist, Kiara, would have a heart attack if she ever found out. But Kiara had never been in her shoes. She'd never needed to keep her son safe from goons who wanted to kill him.

She picked up the scissors and met her reflection in the mirror. Her long blond hair lay draped over her shoulders like a shroud. Her crowning glory, as her mother would often tout. Steven used to say her hair was gold in his pocket because with her by his side he could never lose.

But her hair no longer mattered. It was a symbol of her old life. A life lived to please others. Beauty pageant judges, her mother, Steven.

No more. She would no longer allow herself to be the trophy daughter. The trophy wife. She was Vivian, Mikey's mother.

Grabbing a hunk of hair, she began to saw away the invisible shackles of oppression. From this day forward she would be in charge of her life.

No one would ever take her freedom or her choices away from her again.

Anthony took his time checking on the thankfully sleeping boy. The warmth and fierce protectiveness coursing through him was more than a complication. It was a disaster.

When he returned to his room, the bathroom door was closed again. He leaned against the wall to wait; willing himself not to let her affect him again. He had to keep himself immune to her charms.

A few moments later, the bathroom door opened. He stepped inside and sucked in a sharp breath.

FIVE

The polished beauty queen was gone.

Vivian had cut her hair. She'd cut it *short*. In choppy layers, the longest of which skimmed her brows, ears and the delicate nape of her neck. Huge chunks of her silky tresses lay scattered on the floor.

Anthony liked the pixie look on her. The way her hair now framed her face accentuated her big blue eyes and the long column of her slender throat. She'd scrubbed her face clean of any makeup, leaving her fresh-faced and oh, so appealing. His blood revved like the engine on an Indy 500 car.

He was tempted to stop here and not use the dye. But her unique shade of white-blonde would still give her away.

She touched the sheared ends. "I've never had short hair." A soft, bemused smile played at the corners of her pretty mouth. "It feels so…light."

Drawn to her like a man in a drought and she were the proverbial oasis, he stepped closer. "You look good. Really good," he said, meeting her gaze in the mirror's reflection.

The vulnerability in her eyes tore at his heart. "It needs a bit of shaping. I couldn't quite get the back."

"I can help with that." He picked up the shears lying on the counter. He was surprised to notice his hand shake. Taking a deep calming breath, he waited a second for control to return. When his hand was steady, he trimmed the wayward strands she'd missed and evened out a few places. "There. Perfect."

Mirth danced in her lovely eyes. "Nice job. Have you ever considered becoming a stylist?"

He scoffed. "No. And don't tell my siblings, or I'll never hear the end of it."

"You have siblings?"

The wistful note in her voice touched him. "Yes. A brother and a sister. I'm the eldest."

Turning to face him, she asked, "Do you get along with them?"

"I do." He opened the box of dye and pulled out the contents. "We're pretty close-knit."

Longing entered her gaze. "I always wanted

a sister. Or a brother. I wanted that for Mikey, too, but Steven…didn't."

"It's not too late."

Her gaze lifted to his. "True. Maybe one day. But…" She turned back toward the sink and worked at mixing the dye with the activating solution. "I'd have to adopt because I don't think I'll ever remarry. Just the thought of being that subjugated again to someone else makes my skin crawl."

Though he ached for her pain, he couldn't let her believe that what she'd experienced was the norm. "Not all marriages are like yours. My parents have been married for nearly forty-five years. Yeah, they've fought and had their difficult moments, but they would die for each other. Die *without* each other."

"I think that's rare. My parents tolerate each other, at best."

"Relationships are what you make of them."

She titled her head and looked at him through the mirror. "What about you? Are you married?"

He shook his head, a dull ache throbbing in his chest.

"Ever come close?"

Regret colored his words. "Yes. Once."

"What happened?"

"My life was derailed and she got tired of waiting for me to get my act together." Or more specifically tired of him putting off setting a date.

"The assassination?"

He nodded.

"You've got your life together now, right? Why not find out if she'd take you back?"

The pointed question caught him off guard. He didn't have an answer. The thought had never occurred to him.

"Don't rule out reconciliation until you've tried," Vivian said, softly.

The idea bounced around his mind but wouldn't take root. "I suppose you're right. Something to at least consider when this assignment's over."

He tried to decipher how he felt about pursuing Becca again, but with Vivian so close, her fresh scent filling his head and her bright blue eyes watching him, he could hardly breathe properly, let alone think.

Abruptly, Viv pushed the container of dye into his chest. "Let's get this done."

Closing his hand over hers, he took the bottle. Heat from her hand raced up his arm and spread across his chest. She jerked her hand away. She moved to lean her head over the sink. Taking a deep bracing breath,

Anthony adjusted the towel over her shoulders to protect her neck and the T-shirt from the purple-colored liquid. Gently he worked the dye through the short strands, trying not to let the intimacy of having his hands in her hair get to him.

He kept his gaze focused on her hair and not where the hem of the T-shirt rose above her knees. Sweat beaded on Anthony's brow.

"Okay, all the gunk is gone from the bottle. Now what?"

"It sits for fifteen minutes."

Anthony checked the time on his watch. She took a seat on the edge of the tub to wait for the color to set.

Needing some space, Anthony said, "I'll check on Mikey and be back in fifteen."

Her pleased smile zinged straight through him. He beat a hasty retreat. Pausing between rooms, he leaned his forehead against the doorjamb. He'd revealed more than he'd intended and felt way more than he wanted to. He had to put a halt to the attraction and connection building between him and Vivian. She was his protectee. His client. Nothing more. There couldn't be anything more.

He moved into the connecting room and leaned against the wall. Mikey slept peacefully in the bed. Unfamiliar emotions rose.

Anthony had never been responsible for a child's life before. Diplomats and their wives and presidents and first ladies, but never a child this young. There was something so innocent about Mikey. Anthony supposed the coping disorder made the child seem even more in need of protecting.

He returned to Viv. "Time's up. Hey, cutting Mikey's hair might be enough of a change and less traumatic for him."

The tender look of approval in Viv's blue eyes shot straight to Anthony's core, knocking him off balance.

"Thank you," she said softly. "Just give me a few minutes to rinse."

Taking the scissors with him, Anthony walked out and shut the bathroom door behind him.

Vivian blinked back tears. Anthony's consideration for her son touched her deeply. The more she got to know Anthony the more she was finding herself drawn to him.

Her *bodyguard*.

Of course the intense situation exaggerated her feelings. The close proximity and the need to rely on him for her and Mikey's safety warped her sense of reality. Once this was over, once she didn't have to live in fear of being hunted down and killed or sent to prison for a crime she didn't commit, she'd be able to look rationally at her emotions.

For now she'd be grateful for the kindness and compassion Anthony showed to both her and her son. There was no harm in being thankful and appreciative. She just couldn't allow anything else to develop.

Though why the thought of Anthony with another woman made her stomach knot, she didn't know. Silliness on her part. She didn't care who his future was with as long as he kept her and Mikey safe.

After rinsing out the dye in the shower and then blow-drying her hair with the hotel's dryer, she put back on her sweater and slacks. She hardly recognized herself in the mirror's reflection. The dark hair was so shockingly different. She hoped Mikey didn't freak out when he saw her.

First they had to cut Mikey's dark curls. She joined Anthony at Mikey's beside. The table lamp cast a soft glow in the room.

"Wow." Anthony's stunned expression unnerved her.

She touched her hair. "That bad, huh?"

"You were gorgeous as a blonde, but as a brunette, you're stunning. The dark hair with your pale skin and pale eyes is…amazing."

Heat flamed her cheeks. She couldn't

detect any hidden agenda in his tone or in the sincere expression on his handsome face. And for some reason his compliment didn't infuriate her as most compliments on her looks usually did.

She rather liked the idea that Anthony Carlucci, bodyguard extraordinaire, thought she was gorgeous and stunning. Too bad it could never lead anywhere.

Taking a seat beside her sleeping son, she gathered him in her arms. Mikey stirred slightly. She made soothing noises to settle him until his slim body relaxed against her. Her heart overflowed with love as she held him while Anthony cut at the thick hair covering Mikey's head. Before long, her son had very short hair. She hadn't realized how young he'd looked with his curls. She settled him back against the pillow.

Headlights in the parking lot swept past the lightweight curtains. Anthony rose and went to the window. He pushed back the curtain slightly and peered out. His frown sent apprehension sliding over Viv's limbs.

Moving to his side, she asked, "What's wrong?"

"Turn out the lights," he replied in a hushed tone.

Heart thumping, she quickly turned out the

bedside lamp, throwing the room into semi-darkness. Light from the parking lot filtered through the curtains. Anthony stayed at the window, watching.

Anthony made a disgusted noise. "How did they find us?"

Viv's stomach sank. She ran to the window. "Let me see."

He stepped back. She peered out the slit in the curtain. Below in the parking lot two men were climbing out of a black SUV. She sucked in a sharp breath and stumbled back. Shock ricocheted through her. "Those are the FBI agents I was telling you about."

Her gaze flew to Anthony. She'd trusted him to keep them safe. How could this be happening?

Anthony scooped Mikey up and carried him toward the connecting room. She dogged his steps. He set Mikey on the bathroom floor. "Stay here. Lock the door."

Fear slammed against her ribs as she twisted the lock behind Anthony. Feeling alone and vulnerable, she scooted over to Mikey. She loved him so much. She couldn't bear the thought of anything happening to her son. Gathering him in her arms, she closed her eyes and prayed.

* * *

Adrenaline pumped through Anthony's veins. He grabbed his SIG Sauer P229 from his holster hanging over the back of a chair. He checked the slide, extinguished the bedside lamp and moved quickly into the room Viv and Mikey shared. He closed the connecting door and rushed to the window.

Two men, weapons drawn, made their way up the stairs. Shadows obstructed their faces. The men stopped on the landing to check a small glowing gadget one of them was holding before stalking forward and stopping in front of the door to Anthony's room.

He reared back. They had some sort of tracking device.

Anger and fear tightened his chest. His mind raced. One thought formed. Stop the men before they could get to Viv and Mikey. Whether Viv was involved in her husband's murder or not, Anthony had to make sure they stayed alive. That's what he'd been hired to do. Trained to do. He couldn't fail again.

He had to act fast. He moved to the bed, swiped one of the dense fiber-filled pillows and rushed back through the connecting door. Two seconds later the outer door burst open. Leading with their guns, the two men entered the darkened room.

This better work. With the pillow over the barrel of his gun as a makeshift silencer, Anthony fired, hitting the first man in the thigh. A scream of surprise and pain echoed through the room.

The bright flash from a muzzle and the distinct "psst" noise of a silencer alerted Anthony to incoming fire. He rolled sideways as a slug slammed into the wall where he'd just been. He brought the pillow and barrel up to shoot the second assailant in the shoulder. The man went down with a cry.

Anthony made quick work of disarming the wounded assassins. They refused to answer his questions. He yanked the sheet from the bed and ripped it into strips to use as binding and to dress their wounds. He didn't want them bleeding out before they were found. After tying the men's hands and feet together, he dragged them into the closet and shut the door. He wedged a chair against the handle to lock them inside.

Relieved, yet knowing there could be others on their way, Anthony hustled to get Viv and Mikey. Breathing hard from adrenaline, he opened the bathroom door and flipped on the light switch.

Viv and Mikey were huddled in the corner. Viv used her body to shield her son, even though her eyes were scrunched closed. The instincts of a mother. Tenderness welled.

Her pale skin and tight mouth showed her terror. His heart melted a little more each time she tried to be strong for her son no matter how scared she really was. He wanted to take all her fear away. Kneeling beside her, he laid a hand on her shoulder. She jerked with a whimper.

"Shhh. It's okay. It's me," he said.

She opened her eyes. Relief and trust shone bright in her gaze. His heart squeezed tight.

She peered over his shoulder. "I heard… noises."

"I neutralized the threat. But we have to go." He helped her to her feet.

Mikey awoke and struggled to be let go. He took one look at his mother, his gaze skipping to her dark hair and began to scream.

Viv clapped a hand over his mouth. "Shh, baby. Quiet now. It's all right. Everything's all right."

Anthony smoothed a hand over his shorn hair. "Your mom looks different. But it's her, okay?"

Mikey calmed and touched a hand to Viv's face. She smiled encouragingly. He seemed to accept her new look.

"We need to go," Anthony said, ushering

them out of the confines of the bathroom. "There might be others coming."

Viv held on tight to Mikey and guided him through the connecting door. Anthony grabbed his things and all the discarded trash from their earlier activities. No time to wipe down the rooms. Every second they remained here put them at risk. With all the noise, the police were no doubt on their way. And there could still be more bad guys coming.

He shut the connecting door and locked it. "We can't leave anything behind. Not even the trash. Nothing that will tell them we've dyed your hair or cut his."

Together they picked up as much as they could.

"Time to move."

Anthony went out first to make sure it was safe before waving Viv to follow. Viv had her hands full coaxing Mikey down the stairs. Anthony urged them to the back of the parking lot where he'd parked the van. Once they'd stowed their stuff and gotten in the van, Viv started a DVD for Mikey.

Anthony didn't fire up the engine. Instead, he held up the device he'd taken from the assassins. "They have some way of tracking you that led them straight here. We can't make a move until we figure out what it is."

Anthony grabbed Viv's bag from the floorboard at her feet. He dug around inside. He pushed aside the leather wallet, a bottle of perfume, and a pack of gum and a handful of hard candy. His hand closed around a small Taser.

Wary surprise rocketed through him. He held the Taser up. "You didn't tell me you had this."

She shrugged. "You didn't ask."

Doubts filtered through his mind. What else was she hiding?

He set the Taser aside and reached back inside the bag.

He brought out a four-by-four-inch rectangular black unit with an LED screen showing a tiny green blip. "What's this?"

"The monitor for Mikey's Wanderer Alert ankle bracelet." She twisted around to reach back and tugged Mikey's pant leg up to reveal a white strap with a square head that glowed green. "He's escaped from the house a few times."

Frustration beat a bass drum behind Anthony's eyes. "Didn't think to mention that either."

No wonder they kept being found. Until this very moment he hadn't realized how afraid he was that he'd lost his edge, his ability to protect.

"No one knows he wears it," she stated.

Arching an eyebrow, Anthony said, "Someone does."

She frowned. "Well, of course a few people do. I meant the public at large. Steven was careful to keep Mikey's autism out of the media."

"Then who?"

"The staff. Mikey's teachers, a few close friends and associates of Steven's, but none of them would… I mean, I can't believe…" Her complexion lost even more color.

"Believe it. Someone not only knows Mikey wears the bracelet, but has the capability to hack into his signal." And the means to hire assassins.

Anthony grabbed the scissors from the console tray where he'd placed them. "The bracelet has got to go."

Distress pinched the corners of her mouth as she wrestled with his proclamation. Finally, she nodded. "You're right, of course. I'll distract him while you cut."

Anthony slipped out of the driver's seat, opened the back panel door and scooted next to Mikey.

"Honey, are you hungry?" Viv said. "Would you like a snack?"

Mikey pointed at the screen. "Watching."

Leaning in, Anthony snipped the strap attached to Mikey's ankle. It fell to the floor. Taking the strap and the monitor, he retreated, shutting the door firmly. He looked around the parking lot, his gaze landing on the big rig a few feet away. Quickly he darted to the truck, worked the tie holding the tarp over the cargo bed until he had a corner lose enough to slip the monitor and bracelet inside. He retied the tarp down tight and jogged back to the van.

Once they were on the road, he said, "I need you to write down every person who knows about the Wanderer Alert bracelet."

Her shoulders sagged. A tear crested her lashes. "I hate thinking someone I know and trust could have killed Steven. It just doesn't seem possible."

Feeling her pain as acutely as if he'd been the one betrayed, Anthony said, "We can never be sure what lies in another person's heart."

"I know you're right," she replied and wiped at the tears. She dug into her bag and produced a notepad and pen. "It will be a short list."

"Easier to find who's behind your husband's murder and who wants you and Mikey dead."

"Now do you believe me that I had nothing to do with Steven's murder?"

Her voice dropped to a whisper on the last word, but the note of hope in her tone and the plea in her big baby-blues were clearly identifiable.

Anthony's gut clenched. Was he ready to believe in her innocence?

SIX

Anthony searched his heart. Though he'd only been with Vivian a short time, he was sure she wouldn't do anything to deliberately put Mikey in harm's way. Her love for her son was undeniable.

And he liked that about her. In fact, he really liked her. He admired her faith, admired her sacrifices for the sake of her child, admired her intelligence and her quick thinking. He was attracted too, but that didn't weigh in on the realization he no longer considered her a suspect in the senator's murder. She was as much a victim as her husband.

"I do believe you."

"About time." She visibly straightened her spine and proceeded to make the list of possible suspects. Respect for this tough lady spread through him. He would make sure she didn't end up dead, too. And not just because it was his job.

* * *

They stopped at a roadside diner. While Viv and Mikey stayed within the safety of the van, Anthony ordered their breakfasts to go. They ate in the parking lot, behind a big rig so no one would see the van.

Pancakes, eggs and bacon. All of Mikey's favorites. Viv ate, but her appetite wasn't big. She noticed Anthony wasn't particularly hungry either.

Probably still upset with her for not mentioning the Wanderer Alert. She hadn't considered that whomever was after her would know about the monitoring device, let alone be able to circumvent the security of the Wanderer Alert company's computer system.

At least Anthony no longer doubted her innocence. Having him fully on her side bolstered her confidence that they would arrive in Boston safely.

And the delegate from Kashmir probably had been just as confident that he'd be protected. Viv pushed away that unsettling thought as she pushed away her half-eaten plate.

She had to trust that God would keep her and Mikey safe. Through Anthony.

As they finished up their breakfast and stored the containers in the back, Viv could tell Anthony needed to rest, but he shook off her offer to drive.

"I'll be fine," he insisted. Though he'd ordered a large coffee to go, as well.

Stubborn man. "You'll be no good to me or Mikey if you push yourself to exhaustion," Viv argued.

"We'll stop again in a few hours. I want to put some more distance between us and…"

She nodded knowing exactly who he meant. The two men sent to kill her and Mikey. A shiver ran down her spine. "Did you…"

"Kill them?" He shook his head. "No. Just flesh wounds."

She was impressed by his restraint, his mercy.

Four hours later, Anthony slowed the van down and turned into the parking lot of a large mall. "We need new clothes."

"You'll get no argument from me on that," Viv said, adjusting her ball cap.

She promised Mikey a toy so he would cooperate by wearing the ball cap and sunglasses as they entered a large department store. Time flew as Viv, with Anthony's help, collected a few comfortable outfits for her and Mikey. If anyone thought it strange that they were in their hats and shades inside, no one commented. In the toy department she'd found a few puzzles and a Rubik's Cube for Mikey, things that would keep him busy during their trip.

She stopped by the cosmetic department where she picked up a few toiletry items and then led both Mikey and Anthony to the men's department.

She helped Anthony gather a couple of outfits—soft-looking jeans, graphic T-shirts and a nice polo shirt. Clothes Steven would have sneered at. When they took their armload of clothes to the checkout counter, Anthony stopped Viv from using her credit card.

"Too easy for someone to trace," he murmured as he removed a card from his own wallet and handed it to the clerk.

Concern arched through her. When their transaction was completed and they were headed back toward the car, she asked, "And they couldn't trace your credit card? Surely whoever is after me knows about you."

"It's a loaded cash card," he said. He opened the back of the van and stowed away their packages. "Trent gives each of his operatives one. There's no way to trace the user of the card."

"That's good to know." Her father had been right to hire Trent Associates. Competent, smart and worth every cent.

She started back toward the passenger seat when Anthony snagged her elbow. His big hand warm on her skin. She lifted her gaze and met his. Dark circles rimmed his rich chocolate-colored eyes.

He held out the keys. "I'll take you up on that offer. I need a half hour of downtime."

Thrilled to be of use, she held out her hand. Steven never let her drive when they were going anywhere together. He always had to be in control. "Thank you."

Placing the keys in her open palm but not releasing his hold, he said, "A couple things. I want you to be aware of the cars behind you. If you even think we're being followed, you let me know."

"Okay." She bit her lip as nervousness vied with excitement. His trust meant a great deal. "Uh, how will I know if a car is following us specifically? I mean, we'll be on a freeway and I can't imagine I'll know a bad guy from anyone else."

He closed his hand over hers, the pressure sending little tingles up her arm that heightened the nervous excitement playing havoc with her system.

"If a car stays in position behind you for any length of time, change lanes," he instructed. "If they change too and stay the same distance behind you, they're most likely following. It could be nothing. It could be something. Trust your instincts. If you feel funny about anything, pull off and I'll take over."

"Okay." Squaring her shoulders, she said, "I can do this."

"I know you can."

The confident smile he gave her filled her with pleasure. She really appreciated being treated like a competent person.

Behind the wheel, Viv maneuvered out of the mall and onto the interstate. Mikey went back to watching a video while his hands worked the Rubik's Cube. She was so proud of him. He'd handled all the stress better than she could have imagined. Of course, allowing him so much television went against everything she believed, but considering the situation, having videos to occupy him made the trip bearable.

As did the man reclining in the passenger seat.

He was on his cell phone giving someone named Simone at Trent Associates the names from the list she'd made of people aware of Mikey's Wanderer Alert bracelet.

Though the thought of one of those people betraying her and Mikey made her heart hurt, affection for the man trying to keep them safe soothed the ache. His compassion and kindness to both her and Mikey in the face of danger said a lot about his honor and integrity.

He could have easily belittled her for not realizing the Wanderer Alert was a means of tracking them, but he wasn't a man who abused his power. He was a man worthy of admiration and respect. Of caring.

She told herself not to let herself get too attached or put too much weight on the emotion spreading through her. His heart was already spoken for and she…she didn't want anyone. Ever again. Right?

They stopped for the night in Nebraska. Instead of connecting rooms, this time Anthony got one room. Since he'd managed to catch a few z's on the road, he sat in a chair by the window standing guard while Viv and Mikey slept. In the quiet of the night, he found himself talking to God. Not praying, necessarily. Just silently conversing like he used to as a kid. The one-sided conversation kept him alert but also eased something in his soul.

Knowing it was better to leave while the other hotel guests were still asleep, he awoke Viv before sunrise. Less likely for anyone to remember seeing them that way. He carried

Mikey to the van while Viv brought their things. Halfway to the vehicle, Mikey stirred. Lifting his head, his gaze touched Anthony's face before averting off to the side.

Anthony braced himself, expecting the kid to scream to be let go but amazingly, Mikey reached up to touch his face before laying his head back against Anthony's shoulder.

Tenderness inundated Anthony, making his throat burn. He met Viv's tear-filled gaze. She radiated trust and fondness. *Uh, oh. Not good.*

The last thing he wanted was her thinking of him as daddy material. Even though she'd vowed she wouldn't remarry, he knew enough about her to know she'd do anything for Mikey. But Anthony wasn't ready to be a father. Or a husband, for that matter.

And that realization gave him pause. Was that why he hadn't chased after Becca?

Stowing the question to the back of his mind, he strode to the van. After securing Mikey in the back, Anthony rounded the van and found Viv by the driver's door.

"That was amazing," she said in a soft voice. "He likes you."

Swallowing past the lump in his throat, Anthony reached for the door. "He's getting used to me, is all."

Skepticism flashed in Viv's blue eyes. "If that's what you want to believe."

He didn't want to think about it. "We should get going."

She blew out a breath before going around to the other side of the van and getting in. Silent tension filled the van as the miles went by. Anthony couldn't help noticing how cute Viv looked in the jeans and the flowered long-sleeved blouse she'd bought. He forced his gaze back to the road. He couldn't fix it because he didn't know what to say, how he could explain why he wasn't the right guy for her or Mikey. Could never be even if he wanted to, because he didn't have what it took, what she needed, what a woman like her and a kid like Mikey deserved.

When they hit the state of Iowa around noon, Viv asked if they could stop for lunch.

"Sure, we'll find a drive-through up ahead," Anthony said as he took the next exit.

"Okay, but can we eat in a park of some kind? I need to stretch my legs and get some fresh air. And so does Mikey."

"If there's one close," he promised. The fast-food clerk gave him directions to a nearby park in a residential neighborhood. Anthony parked at the curb. Wearing their hats and sunglasses, they climbed out of the van.

As soon as Viv released Mikey, he squealed with delight, "Play!" He took off across the grass toward a solid wooden play structure complete with slides and swings.

Viv watched him with a soft smile. "He loves swings. I should go after him."

Anthony's gaze swept the park, looking for anyone who might be a threat. The oblong park was flanked on all sides by picturesque homes. A few other children played on the structure while their mothers or nannies sat on a bench, talking. A couple played Frisbee in the middle of a lush green lawn, a woman walked a toddler in a stroller along the sidewalk that rimmed the park at the far end and an elderly man with an English bulldog on a leash crossed the street to enter the park. The neighborhood appeared safe enough. And if anyone entered the park they would be easily spotted.

"He should be okay for a moment." He gestured toward an empty picnic table. "Let's set up over there."

They walked to the table. Viv laid out several napkins like a tablecloth. Anthony took out the hamburgers and fries and set the drinks on the table.

"I'll get Mikey." Viv walked away toward the play area, leaving her sunglasses on the table.

Shifting his attention away from Viv, Anthony's gaze swept the park once again. He popped a fry into his mouth and could feel the grease congealing in his veins even before he swallowed. He longed for some of his mother's home cooking. Manicotti bursting with ricotta cheese and a zesty tomato sauce, vegetable frittata loaded with fresh veggies from her garden boxes or her tiramisu with rich chocolate and mascarpone over espresso-soaked ladyfingers.

"Anthony!"

Viv's desperate cry tore him from his thoughts. She stood near the structure. Even from this distance he could see the panic on her lovely face. Dread slashed through him. Something was wrong. He jumped up and ran to her.

Taking her by the shoulders, he stared into her eyes. "Steady now. What's the matter? Where's Mikey?"

She could barely get the words out. "He's gone."

Anthony's stomach dropped. "He's got to be here somewhere."

"What if they got him!" She yanked out of

his grasp. "I should have kept a closer eye on him. I just thought we were finally safe."

Feelings of failure, of inadequacy, reached up to choke Anthony. Could he have missed a tail? Had the bad guys found them again? No. He would have seen them. They would have drawn his attention.

He forced himself to think clearly, calmly. "Maybe he's hiding in the play structure or went to the restroom." He gestured toward the building at the other end of the park, the only blind spot.

They searched the structure. Anthony asked the women sitting on the bench if they'd seen Mikey.

"I didn't see where he wandered off to," one of the women said. "We'll help you look."

The three women gathered their children and then spread out, calling for Mikey. Viv and Anthony ran to the restroom. He wasn't there.

"Mikey!" Desperation rang in Viv's tone.

Anthony winced, but knew that at the moment, it was more important to find Mikey than keep a low profile.

Movement near the porch of a house across the street from the park caught Anthony's attention. For a split second he was sure he'd seen Mikey. Taking Viv by the elbow, Anthony steered her toward the yellow house with its wide front staircase and wraparound porch. A noise drew them to the right side of the stairs. Mikey had wiggled halfway under the porch, his legs and feet pushing against the ground. Relief crashed over Anthony. He couldn't decide if the kid was trying to wedge himself in farther or was trying to get unstuck from the tight space between the wood and the ground.

Viv rushed forward. She squatted beside the boy and tugged him free. "Mikey, what on earth are you doing?"

When he came out, he was holding an orange tabby cat. Mikey smiled triumphantly. "Kitty!"

Hugging her son close, Viv began to cry. "You scared Mommy."

Mikey frowned and touched Viv's wet cheek. "No cry."

Viv's eyes widened and then softened into a loving gaze. Anthony's blood pounded in his ears. The purity of Viv's love for her son heightened her beauty way beyond the mere physical and touched Anthony's heart.

"We need to let the kitty go," Viv said. "He has a home to go to." She helped Mikey to release the cat, who darted back under the porch.

Anthony held out his hand for Viv, intending to help her up, but Mikey slipped his hand into Anthony's larger one. Surprise and something else, something foreign, exploded in his chest. Anthony held his other hand out to Viv. She gazed at him with such trust and affection he thought he might bust.

She grasped his hand and he pulled her to her feet. She held on as the three of them walked back to the park. From the outside Anthony knew they appeared to be a family, connected by hands, by love. A father, mother and son.

The thought sent his heart galloping. He was becoming attached to his protectees. Not a good thing. Very dangerous.

One of the first rules of protection was: don't get involved. Doing so impaired the protector's ability to make objective decisions.

By the time they reached the picnic table, rational thought returned. These two people were his clients. Not his family. He had a job to do. Nothing more.

Though the food had gone cold, Mikey didn't seem to mind as he ate his burger and started on the fries. Anthony had lost his appetite and apparently so had Viv. Their food lay untouched.

Viv reached over to caress his hand. Her

soft skin felt so good against his own. "I'm sorry I got a little hysterical."

Despite knowing how he should behave, he turned his hand over and captured hers, entwining their fingers. The responsibility of caring for these two people weighed heavily on his shoulders. If something happened to them…

He could deny his feelings until doomsday but he was beginning to care more than he should. More than was warranted. If he weren't careful he'd find himself wishing they were a real family. And that terrified him. They were in danger and he had to do what was best for them. Not what he wanted.

He lightly ran his thumb along hers and tried to pull his hand away. She wouldn't let him.

"You were scared," he said. "I was scared, too." He paused. Heart thumping at lightning speed, he had to make a decision. The best decision for them. "It would be better if I have Trent send someone else to escort you the rest of the way."

Viv squeezed his hand. "No way. I don't want anyone else. We don't want anyone else. Mikey trusts you. You don't know how rare that is."

His gut clenched. He wasn't willing to live

with the consequences if something were to go wrong. "I told you what happened to the last person who trusted me to keep them safe."

Her gaze narrowed. "What was the saying your superiors used? 'If a bullet's got your name on it there's nothing anyone can do.' And what did you tell me that meant?" Without waiting for him to answer, she continued, "It means even the best sometimes can't stop the inevitable."

"But I'm not the best," he argued. "Not by a long shot."

Determination lit her eyes. Her chin lifted in a show of stubborn defiance. "You're the best for us. And I know God is with us. He's been with us from the beginning."

Anthony blew out a breath, wishing he believed God was with them. Yet, looking at Viv and Mikey, knowing their story, knowing how deeply her faith went, Anthony found himself hoping she was right.

If only they knew who was after them.

Anthony's gaze shifted to Mikey. The kid had witnessed his father's murder from beneath the desk. Could he really identify the killer?

And if he could, that would be the only thing that would keep them safe.

"Vivian, we need to know what Mikey knows."

SEVEN

Failure! Rage seethed in the man's veins. The two wounded operatives were found by the hotel maid trussed up like turkeys on Thanksgiving. The woman and child had escaped. The Wanderer Alert bracelet had been removed from the boy and sent on a wild goose chase to California. How much more incompetence could he take?

His hands fisted. His gaze zeroed in on his assistant. Wendell's flushed face and anxious gaze fueled the man's anger. "Tell me you have a plan," he ground out.

Wendell blinked, his head bobbing. "Yes, sir. I've people watching everyone who Mrs. Grant might contact, plus I have men stationed outside Trent Associates' headquarters in Boston. That seems the most logical place for them to go."

The man grunted his approval and spun away. He stalked to the window to stare out at the view of the Washington Monument. "What do we know about this bodyguard?"

"Name's Anthony Carlucci, *ex-Secret Service*." Wendell delivered the credential like the bomb it was. Now they knew they were facing an additional skill set that could be game changing. "A year ago he took a bullet in the line of duty while protecting a delegate from Kashmir."

"Ah, yes. I remember the incident." He'd been in attendance at the state function when a man dressed as a caterer had delivered a fatal shot to the delegate. Carlucci had unsuccessfully tried to intervene. Just another example of incompetence. "Do we have anyone in Secret Service?"

"Yes, sir."

"Good. Make contact. If Carlucci reaches out, I want to know."

"Sir, are you sure eliminating Mrs. Grant and her son is necessary? I mean, if the boy knew something, wouldn't it be out by now?"

Gut twisting with anxiety, he replied, "I can't take that chance."

"I've tried." The noises of the park receded to white noise as tension stiffened the muscles in Viv's shoulders. "Whatever he saw is locked up inside his head."

Anthony squeezed her hand. "Let me try. He responds to me."

She couldn't deny that. Mikey was receptive to Anthony in a way she hadn't seen before.

Would Anthony's questions do more damage than good to her son?

But did they have a choice?

Anxiety twisted her thoughts. On one hand she hoped Mikey would reveal something, anything that would set them free from the stress of being hunted like wild animals. Yet her heart ached to think of the horror of what he'd seen. No child should have to witness their father's murder. "Okay. Be patient with him."

He gave her an odd look. "Of course." He focused on Mikey. "Mikey, do you remember the last time you saw your father?"

Vivian held her breath. Pressure built in her chest.

Mikey stilled, a French fry halfway to his mouth.

"You were in your bed," Anthony continued, his modulated tone soothing. "You got up and went downstairs. What did you see?"

Mikey's fingers tightened on the fry. Potato squished out the sides.

Protective instincts surged, setting her teeth on edge. She wanted to tell Anthony to stop, not to push Mikey, but she understood how important it was to know what Mikey had witnessed. Empathy tore her up inside. But so much hinged on his answer. "It's okay, baby," she said. "Take your time."

Anthony released his hold on Vivian to cover Mikey's free hand with his own. "You went to the study. Your daddy was working at his desk."

Mikey dropped the fry and began to rock. *Oh, no.* This wasn't good. Any minute he could lose it completely. The urge to draw her son into her arms gripped Viv. Every mothering impulse cried out to hold Mikey, to calm him, to protect him. She had to sit on her hands to keep from reaching for him. Trying to contain him would only make him more agitated. But she longed to shield him. She didn't want him to suffer through the memory of his father's death. She couldn't. It was too late for that now. Their safety— their very lives—depended on what Mikey could remember.

"Not allowed," Mikey said in perfect imitation of Steven's voice.

Viv drew in a sharp breath. Though she'd heard Mikey imitate cartoon characters, he'd never mimicked his father before.

"Your daddy said you were not allowed in the study," Anthony said encouragingly. "Was there someone else in there?"

"Hide," Mikey said, again in a voice eerily like Steven's.

The implication of the word rocketed through Viv. Steven had protected Mikey. For all her husband's faults, he'd done a noble thing when it counted the most. Tears gathered at the corners of her eyes.

"You hid under the desk?" Anthony pressed. "Someone came into the room?"

Mikey began to make a noise deep in his throat.

Viv recognized the noise. She winced. "Whenever Steven would raise his voice, Mikey would make this sound," she said to Anthony.

Meeting her gaze, he nodded. To Mikey he said, "Your daddy was talking loudly. Arguing with someone. Did you see the person?"

Mikey shook his head. Then puffed up his chest, taking on a different posture. "You can't blackmail me."

Floored, Viv stared. The words were shocking enough, but the voice Mikey imitated wasn't Steven's.

Blackmail? Anger underscored her shock. Whatever illicit scheme Steven had been involved with had been his downfall. And could very well get his son killed.

"Do you recognize that voice?" Anthony questioned Viv.

She searched her memory. And came up empty. "It's vaguely familiar but I can't place it."

"Keep thinking. Hopefully you'll remember." Anthony picked up a fry and handed it to Mikey. "Good job, buddy. You did real well."

Mikey snatched the fry and shoved it into his mouth. Then he picked up another fry and offered it to Anthony. With a wry smile Anthony leaned forward and took the offering between his teeth and gulped it down, to Mikey's delight.

Viv watched the interplay with a lump of awe in her throat. In such a short time Anthony had connected to Mikey in a way she'd seen few people do. Adoration spread through her chest. Anthony met her gaze. The tenderness there threatened to melt her heart. But as their gazes touched his expression shifted; his dark eyes became as flat and unreadable as onyx. Cold. Distant.

She didn't understand why he was shutting her out. Or why it stung so badly.

"Let's get a move on," Anthony said as he cleared away their garbage from the picnic table and ushered them back to the van.

Pushing aside thoughts of his icy stare, she told herself she was being silly for being upset. Just because he had bonded with Mikey and she was grateful didn't mean anything would or should develop between her and Anthony. She had to keep her focus on staying alive, not on her growing attachment to him.

Acting on her growing attraction to her bodyguard was not going to happen.

With that thought firmly in place, she settled in for the long ride ahead. She adjusted her seat to a more comfortable position. At Mikey's insistent plea for air, she rolled down her window.

As soon as they hit the highway, Anthony asked, "Do you have any idea who the senator was blackmailing?"

"No." Her stomach knotted. There was so much about Steven she hadn't known. There had been a time when she'd wanted to share all aspects of his life, but Steven's indifference to her and his rejection of Mikey snuffed out that desire. She'd had a role to play in public but at home they left each other to their own accord. "But if he had anything worth hiding he'd have put it in the house safe."

Anthony slanted her a glance. "And risk you finding it?"

"He doesn't…didn't think I knew about the safe. I've never looked in it, but I have the combination. The contractor who installed the safe gave me a copy not realizing I wasn't supposed to have it."

"I'm sure the police have already looked inside it by now."

"I doubt it. It's well-hidden." The knot in her stomach expanded and tightened in her chest. She dreaded the thought of returning to the Woodley Park house, but if they wanted to get to the bottom of what Steven was involved in and clear her name, they had to go back to D.C. "We need to go there."

"Can't. It's not safe. We'll let the authorities handle it."

"I don't trust the authorities. I can't risk giving whoever is framing me more ammunition. They already have the D.C. police, the FBI and the media in their pocket. The only way I'm going to be able to prove my innocence and protect Mikey is to find out what Steven had, and on whom."

"My job is to get you to safety, not put you in more jeopardy."

"You won't let anything happen to me," she said, a confidence in her voice that was very real.

A muscle ticked in his jaw. His hands flexed on the steering wheel.

"You've evaded the bad guys, confronted them and won and figured out how we were being tracked. You're good at what you do. I trust you."

"Look, this isn't a debate," he said finally. But not, she noticed, until she'd told him most of her reasons for trusting him. "We're not going to D.C."

Bristling at the tone of finality in his voice, she curled her upper lip. "Like it or not, I'm going to find out what's in the safe."

A dark thundercloud of anger advanced across his expression. "Not on my watch, you're not."

Not afraid of his anger, she leveled him with a look and dug in her heels. She was tired of being told what to do. "Then maybe you better call Trent and find someone who *will* take me."

The line of his jaw tightened as he clenched

his back teeth. "When we get to Boston, you can do whatever you want." He ripped out the words impatiently. "But I'm not taking you anywhere near D.C."

"I thought I was the client, not your prisoner," she said, allowing irritation to drip from each word.

He spared her a glance. "Your father's the client."

"Give me your phone so I can call my father and have him tell you to take me to D.C." She held out her hand expectantly.

"What about Mikey?" he asked quietly. "You're willing to put him in harm's way on the off chance of finding something incriminating in your house?"

Her hand lowered. Consternation creased her brow. "That's not fair. You know I don't want anything bad to happen to him. But I also don't want to go to prison or end up dead. Either of which leaves him alone and vulnerable. My parents will put him in a facility if anything happens to me. I can't stand the mere thought."

Anthony ran a hand through his hair. The traffic grew increasingly worse as the day wore on. So did his stress. He understood her need to be proactive and find evidence to clear her name. He really did. But every instinct said no way. "How about this? I call a buddy in the Secret Service. Have him go to the house and check the safe."

"How about you call your buddy and have him meet us at the house? Between the two of you, Mikey and I would be safe."

He shook his head. "I'm not taking you anywhere near there."

"Pull over," she demanded. "I want out. Mikey and I can manage without you."

Though he found her bravado endearing, he had to suppress the ironic laugh threatening to escape. "That's ridiculous. You'd both be dead right now if you'd been on your own."

"Only because they could track us using the Wanderer Alert. There's no way anyone can track us now."

Her teeth tugged on her bottom lip. Her confidence wavered for a flash, enough to flip off his frustration with her like a switch.

Her big blues eyes searched his face. "Right?"

"Yes. Still doesn't mean you're out of the woods yet. Until you're both in protective custody, you'll always be at risk."

"Yeah, except that we could just as easily be at risk while in custody. And that's a fact."

As much as he hated to admit it, she had a point. His gut clenched with apprehension.

Whoever murdered her husband was highly connected. Which meant it would be risky to contact anyone from the Secret Service, regardless that he trusted each agent with his life. And she was right; the only way to really secure her safety was to find out who was pulling the strings.

"Let me think about it," he said.

Her tight, satisfied smile annoyed him. But he really couldn't be mad at her. Not when he admired her spunk. He just hoped it didn't get her killed. He couldn't stand the thought of failing her.

He took the next exit and found a gas station. He pulled into the full-service island. While the attendant filled the tank, Anthony stepped out of the van and called Trent.

"Tell me you're not close," James said, his voice laced with an odd note that sent chills of alarm sliding down Anthony's back.

"We're not close. What's wrong?"

"The townhouse is under surveillance. Your sister's running their pictures through NCIC."

As a homicide detective Angie would have access to the National Crime Information Center's database. "How many are there?"

"Four that we've spotted. They're in rentals procured with bogus credit cards and ID's.

Not sure if they're local or not. Haven't decided yet whether to run them off. Might be better to keep them where we can see them. When you get into town go directly to the FBI field office downtown. Talk to Special Agent Mosely."

Wariness slid over Anthony as he glanced toward the van. Through the front windshield he could see Viv, her light blue gaze watching him. Her words played themselves in his head. *They already have the D.C. police, the FBI and the media in their pocket.* "You trust Mosely?"

"Implicitly."

"Good to know. We got some info from the kid. Seems Grant was blackmailing someone."

"Which got him killed," Trent stated. "Hmm. Does the wife have any ideas who?"

"None. But Vivian's sure if her husband had something worth hiding it would be in the house safe."

"Then the authorities would have it."

"Viv doesn't seem to think so. She claims the safe is well-hidden. She's insisting we go to D.C. and check it out."

"She can get into the safe?"

"So she claims."

"D.C.'s risky."

"Agreed. But it may be the only chance we have of clearing her name."

There was a moment of silence on the other line. "I'll send a team to meet you."

"Not sure that's a good idea. What if they're followed? I have someone in D.C. I can call for backup."

"You make your call. Let me know if you need anything," Trent said. "And Carlucci?"

"Yes, sir."

"Protect your witness. And don't get yourself killed in the process."

"So what have you decided?" Viv asked, anxious to know what their next move would be. Her nerves were tingling with a strange mixture of trepidation and exhilaration. She'd gone head-to-head with Anthony, arguing her point and demanding her way, but ultimately she'd left the decision in his capable hands.

He'd made two phone calls while he'd waited for the gas to fill. Had he made arrangements for someone else to complete the assignment of getting them to safety or was he going to hold the line and take her straight to Boston?

Anthony started the van and headed the vehicle back onto the interstate. "We'll head to D.C."

A bit stunned, Viv sat back. She was gratified he'd listened to her and accepted her change of plans. And yet she was leery of returning to the scene of the crime. They *would* be taking a risk. She would be putting Mikey in danger.

She slanted a glance at Anthony. He had proven himself a proficient and skilled bodyguard. He wouldn't let anything happen to them. She was as sure of that as she was of her faith in God. Between the two, she and Mikey were golden.

They stopped for the night in Ohio. The motel had an indoor heated swimming pool. After a quick run to the nearest one-stop-shopping mega store for swimsuits and a few other necessities, Viv and Mikey stood at the edge of the pool. Anthony had first scoped out the pool, making sure they were alone and that there were no cameras in the pool house. She was thankful Mikey had been able to learn how to swim. They both needed the energy outlet right now. Viv was proud how well Mikey was doing on this road trip. She'd expected more fits from being confined, but he seemed content to watch videos and snack on the dried fruit she'd bought during one of their stops.

Anthony had declined getting in the water, but sat back on a reclining chair with his head resting on his folded arms, looking like an ad from a magazine. All male beauty clothed in snug jeans; a red T-shirt that showed off his muscular shoulders nicely. A five o'clock shadow darkened his strong jawline and made him even more ruggedly handsome. She doubted he was as relaxed as he looked because his alert gaze kept scanning the parking lot through the big picture window next to the pool-house door.

Mikey hung on to an orange-colored foam noodle provided by the motel. He laughed as he kicked, propelling himself forward to chase her. Hopping to the side through the water to stay just out of his reach, Viv felt alive and safe. For the moment she refused to think about the impending trip to D.C. Instead, she concentrated on having fun with Mikey. They splashed around for a good hour before Mikey grew tired. While he floated on his back, she swam laps.

When she'd done a hundred reps, she stopped and found that Anthony had moved from his lounge chair to the tiled deck of the pool. He'd slipped off his shoes and socks, rolled up his jeans to his knees and put his feet in the water. Mikey bobbed up and down, going under the water and springing back up while hanging on to Anthony's ankles.

Viv's heart constricted tight. They looked so right together. Like they belonged to each other. Father and son. Like Anthony belonged with them. A family. Her husband. His wife.

She squeezed her eyes shut, blocking out the tender scene, and dove under the water where Anthony couldn't see the longing that had to be etched on her face.

Stop it, she silently screamed at herself.

This man was here for one reason and one reason only. To keep them safe. Not become a father and husband. She didn't want a husband.

Mikey needed a father, her heart shot back.

Her lungs burned, forcing her to rise to the surface for air. Taking a gulping breath, she did the only thing she could. She sent up a silent prayer, releasing the burden of longing and need. God would provide what she and Mikey required in this life, when the time was right. Maybe God would put it on her heart to change her mind about remarrying. But for now, she'd settle for being grateful for the blessing of Anthony's attention to Mikey and his willingness to protect them.

That was all that could ever be between them.

"You can hold your breath for a long time," Anthony commented, his dark eyes searching her face. "I was about ready to come in after you."

His concern was sweet and touching and made her feel special. "I grew up with a pool in the backyard."

She climbed out of the water and dried off before slipping her clothes over her swimsuit. Anthony helped Mikey dry off and then the three of them went back to their motel rooms. Viv had insisted they get connecting rooms again so Anthony could rest and not have to sit in a chair all night. He would need his mind and reflexes sharp when they reached D.C.

She'd just finished putting Mikey down, rubbing his back until he fell asleep, when she heard a moan from the adjoining room. A spear of panic pierced her. Her heart jumped and her mind ran through possible disasters. She grabbed the Taser from her bag and then cautiously pushed opened the connecting door, ready to zap a bad guy.

Instead, she locked gazes with a shirtless

Anthony. He sat on the end of the bed, his arm stalled over his head.

She froze. Her pulse skittered and then thundered in her ears. Her gaze raked across his well-defined chest and caught on the nasty-looking scar marring the flesh between his collarbone and left shoulder. Empathy flooded her at the physical sign of injury.

With a wince of pain, he lowered his arm. "You okay?"

She swallowed, her mouth as dry as the desert. "I heard you groan. I thought…I thought something was wrong."

"Sorry. My shoulder's tight today."

She lowered the Taser to her side. "How?"

He grabbed his shirt and pulled it over his head. "Remember I told you about the delegate from Kashmir? The bullet that killed him went through my shoulder first."

Her breath caught. No wonder he felt guilty for the Kashmir official's death. But he'd done what he was supposed to. He'd tried to prevent a death at a cost to himself.

Admiration and respect spread through her along with something else, something powerful and consuming. Affection?

She could admit to that emotion easily enough, but that wasn't what had her head spinning. There was more, so much more, but she shied away from looking too closely. She couldn't. She didn't dare.

Because there was no future in feeling anything else.

And if she kept repeating that often enough she might actually begin to believe it.

She met his gaze again. The intense flame of heat lighting the dark depths quickened her breath. She recognized the look; acknowledged the same smoldering fire burned within her. She wanted to give herself over to the attraction arcing between them. For once in her life she wanted to take, to be impulsive and rebellious. She wanted what she couldn't have.

With a small, wistful sigh she turned and fled, shutting the door firmly behind her. For Mikey's sake.

But deep down she really knew she was doing this for her own sake. Safety.

Her spirit and her heart had been broken by her marriage. She'd survived thanks to Mikey. But she couldn't afford to have that happen again.

EIGHT

The next morning arrived in a brilliant display of sunshine and cloudless blue skies. After a hasty breakfast at a roadside diner, Anthony pulled out onto the highway that would take them to their destination. Seven hours and four-hundred-odd miles later they reached D.C. Anthony rolled his shoulders, trying to work out the knots driving had formed. He squinted. The late-afternoon sun had alrcady started its descent toward the horizon, its shimmering golden rays bounced off the white stone of the Jefferson Memorial.

Bittersweet memories hit Anthony. He'd been so naive when he'd first hit town and caught sight of the many monuments and memorials representing everything he intended to protect. He'd been captivated by the history and sacrifice of the country he'd wanted to serve. Tried to serve.

He'd relocated to D.C. to fulfill a dream. He'd left ten years later in disgrace.

Would returning now with Viv and Mikey redeem him?

Would anything ever make up for the mistake that had not only put an end to his dream but had cost the man he was protecting his life?

It's convenient and easy to blame God.

Viv's words bounced around his mind, making his soul ache.

I cling to Him.

Anthony fought the yearning to cry out to God. He wasn't ready to let go of his anger, to face the truth of his own guilt, the secret he held close.

The traffic signal turned red. As he brought the van to a stop behind a four-door sedan, he mentally put the brakes on his thoughts. Now was not the time to question his path. They had a mission to accomplish. Lives to protect. Being distracted with what couldn't be changed wasn't productive. He chanced a look at Viv in the passenger seat.

Her lush lips were pressed into a tense line. The emerald color of her blouse reflected in her eyes, turning the blue to a pretty shade of teal. She met his gaze, then her gaze quickly skidded away. The anxiousness he saw there tugged at him. She'd been jumpy yet reserved all day. The bruised hue under her eyes made him wince. She'd obviously had trouble sleeping. So had he. His mind had kept reliving those few moments when she'd been standing in the doorway between their rooms, her eyes devouring him, an expression of pure yearning on her lovely face.

His heart hammered in his chest at the memory.

There'd been no mistaking she'd felt the same magnetic pull that pulsed within him. It had taken every ounce of self-control to remain motionless, to not give in to the need to hold her, to wrap his arms around her and draw her close. Thinking about that moment now…his heart picked up speed.

A horn beeped.

He dragged his attention back to the road and shook off Viv's allure. The light had turned green. He stepped on the gas.

But even when he wasn't looking at Viv, the scent of her shampoo wouldn't allow him to forget her. The close quarters and the strain of evading assassins were to blame for the fascination with this particular client. Once they proved her innocent and neutralized the threat to her and Mikey, Anthony knew all these intense feelings bouncing around inside of him would dissipate.

Then he could figure out his future.

For now he had to decide how best to proceed with the task at hand. Viv and Mikey were his responsibility. He wouldn't let them down.

"We'll drive past your house first," he said. "Make sure it's safe."

She looked over her shoulder at her son. "I'm having second thoughts about taking Mikey back there."

Anthony glanced in the rearview mirror to see Mikey's reflection. He'd fallen asleep. His chin rested on his chest, a Rubik's Cube clutched in one hand and his tattered stuffed bear in the other. Tenderness expanded beneath Anthony's ribs.

The boy was holding up well considering he'd been strapped inside the van for three days. Mikey was a good kid, with a kind heart and a curious mind. Though he lacked most interpersonal skills, he wasn't dumb. He'd had no trouble with the many-pieced jigsaw puzzles Viv had bought or with solving the Rubik's Cube time and time again.

"I don't know what other choice we have."

Anthony didn't want to see the boy hurt either, physically or emotionally.

Viv bit her lower lip. "We could take him to his teacher."

"I don't—"

"Barb Jetton would never hurt Mikey. She's been working with him for the past five years."

"Was her name on the list?"

"Yes. But she had little to no contact with Steven."

Anthony changed lanes and pulled to the curb in front of a restaurant. Plastered across the brick side of the building was the face of a baby tiger as part of an advertisement for the National Zoo. Picking up his phone from the console, he said, "I'll check in with Simone. See if Ms. Jetton sent up any red flags."

On the third ring Lisa the receptionist came on the line. "Trent Associates."

"Simone Walker."

"One moment please." She transferred the call.

"This is Simone."

Anthony recognized the sultry tones. "Carlucci here. I need to know what you found out about a woman named Barb Jetton."

"Well, hello to you, too," she said, with a note of humor.

Anthony grimaced. "Sorry. Hi."

"No problem. Just a sec," she said. "Okay, I ran a background check on all the names on the list you gave me. Yep, her name is here. She has no criminal record. There's nothing to indicate she's involved in the senator's murder."

"Okay, good. Any other names pop out?"

"Unfortunately, no."

"Too bad." Anthony pushed away the stab of disappointment. Of course solving this case wouldn't be that easy. "Thanks for checking."

"Hey, we work together as a team here. Let me know if you need anything else."

"I will." He hung up and then handed Viv the phone. "Call the teacher. See if she's willing."

Viv's eyes filled with relief and gratitude. "Thank you."

"But Viv, you need to be prepared. She may believe the news reports and think the worst."

She made the call. Barb was home, and Viv pleaded her case. From the relieved smile on Viv's face, apparently Barb wasn't as convinced by the news reports as Anthony had feared she might be. But more importantly, Barb was more than willing to spend some time with Mikey. Approval loosened his tense shoulders when Viv explained to the woman on the other end of the line they needed to be discreet. Clearly Viv had a supporter on the other end of the call.

Viv directed Anthony to an older, well-maintained high-rise apartment complex at the corner of Sixteenth and Spring Street. They were parked and nearly home free, so to speak, when the wail of a passing ambulance on its way to the nearby hospital startled Mikey awake with a cry before Viv could get him out of the van.

"Shh, sweetie, it's okay," Viv said as she unbuckled the boy. "We're going to see Teacher Barb. You remember Teacher Barb, don't you?"

As Viv got Mikey out of the vehicle, Anthony assessed their surroundings. The apartment complex had a doorman and security cameras near the entrance. His wary gaze roamed the tree-lined street and the small visitor parking lot, looking for threats. Or cops. He didn't see either.

"Story time," Mikey said.

"That's right. Teacher Barb always reads you stories." Viv took him by the hand and started toward the building.

Anthony snagged her elbow. "Remember, the doorman won't recognize you."

She blinked and touched her now dark hair with her free hand. "Right. Thanks."

When they entered the building the doorman rose from behind his desk. The guy was brawny and looked like he could handle himself. The name tag on his red sports coat read Emerson.

"Can I help you?"

"We're here to see Barb Jetton," Viv said.

Anthony assessed the layout. There was a blind spot by the mailboxes. A small sign on the wall indicated the stairwell was around the corner out of the doorman's sight. There was a video screen on the desk showing the garage exit.

"Ms. Jetton just called down," Emerson said. "She's expecting you." He gestured to the hallway. "Take the elevator to the seventh floor. Apartment 708."

"Thanks." Anthony hustled Viv and Mikey to the elevator. Viv coaxed Mikey inside with a piece of hard candy from her purse.

Once the doors slid closed, Mikey began twisting his index finger with his other hand and made a throaty whimper sound.

Concerned, Anthony asked, "Does he do that often?"

"When he's agitated. He doesn't like elevators."

Anthony laid a hand on the boy's thin shoulder. "I don't much like them, either."

As soon as the doors opened on the seventh floor, Mikey bolted, running full speed toward the end of the hall. Apparently, the kid knew exactly where to go. He halted in front of a door and then banged his head against the wood in two short raps.

The door swung open and a young woman with shoulder-length red curly hair and big brown eyes engulfed Mikey in a hug. Though Mikey allowed the contact without protest, his body stiffened and his expression of torture was almost comical.

"Oh, I've missed you these past few days," Barb Jetton said as she released Mikey.

The boy would have darted past his teacher, but Anthony quickly caught him by the elbow. "Wait."

Mikey froze.

Two sets of female eyes turned toward him. To Viv, he said, "I need to clear the place first."

With an understanding nod, Viv drew Barb

out of the way so Anthony could enter. He
made a quick sweep to be sure they weren't
walking into a trap. No matter how much Viv
trusted this woman, he wasn't taking chances.
"All clear." He touched Mikey gently on the
head. "You can go."

The kid darted past him and disappeared
inside.

Barb slanted him a worried look before
turning her attention back to Viv. "Wow. I
hardly recognized you."

Viv touched the short dark ends of her new
hairstyle. The uncertainty on her lovely face
stabbed at Anthony.

"I like it," Barb declared decisively and
pulled Viv into a hug. "Everyone at the school
has been so worried. None of us believe what
they are saying on the news."

Viv eased away, visibly relieved by her
friend's words. "Thank you. And thank you
for taking Mikey."

"Of course," Barb said. Her gaze shot past
Viv and eyed Anthony curiously. She held
out her hand. "Hi. I'm Barb Jetton. And you
are…?"

"Anthony." He gave her petite hand a quick
shake.

"Nice to meet you."

"Does the doorman always vet the residence's guests?" Anthony asked.

Barb nodded. "Oh yes. He's a good watchdog."

That was the answer Anthony hoped for. "Good. Where are the stairs?"

She pointed to her left. "Other end of the hall."

"Any other outside entrances into the building beside the front door?"

"The parking garage entrance connects to the staircase. But you need a code. No one gets in or out without Emerson knowing. If he sees someone that doesn't belong, he's quick to call the police."

"That's good." Anthony handed her a Trent Associates business card. "If we aren't back in two hours, call this number. Ask for James Trent. He'll know what to do. And please, don't tell anyone else about this."

"I won't," Barb replied, her expression grim.

To Viv he said, "We should go."

Viv stepped into the open doorway. "Bye, Mikey. I'll be back soon."

When they were seated in the van, Viv leaned back and closed her eyes. For a moment he thought she was resting, but then he noticed her lips were moving. She was praying. An answering need rose in him.

Okay Lord, for her sake, for Mikey's sake, I have to trust You'll watch over them both. Please.

Vivian realized she'd slid lower in her seat as Anthony circled the block with headlights off even though twilight was making an appearance. The overhead streetlights shone on the wide sidewalks in round pools, leaving obscure dark patches of potential danger. They passed her and Steven's stately redbrick Georgian house twice before Anthony finally parked the van a block away. Viv felt nothing as she gazed at the lonely structure. This part of her life seemed so long ago.

She hadn't seen anything or anyone unusual in her neighborhood as they'd driven through. But she appreciated Anthony's caution.

And she was glad she'd heeded the inner urging to keep Mikey away from the house. At first she'd worried she was being double-minded, but the closer they had traveled to D.C. the more anxious she'd grown. But now she had a sense of peace in regard to Mikey. She'd made the right decision to take him to Barb's.

"This is the plan," Anthony said before she

could climb out of the van. "We're going to go through your neighbor's backyard to get to your house. Do they have a dog?"

"No, but what if they're home? Mary and Len would freak out if they saw us running through their yard." Her neighbors were getting on in years. She didn't want to frighten them unduly.

"We'll think of something. Just keep to the shadows. Hopefully, we can get in and out before anyone even realizes we've been there."

"What if the people who've been after us, you know, the bad guys, are in the house? Or the police have the place staked out?"

Anthony checked his weapon. "We'll deal with it. I don't see any signs of a stakeout, and the crime scene techs would have released the scene by now, so there's no reason to think the police are around."

She tried to hide her flash of doubt. He did this sort of cloak-and-dagger stuff for a living. She had to trust he'd keep her safe. Truth was she did trust him on so many levels. Seeing him with Mikey, watching him protect them on their journey east, she knew he would do all he could.

But the unknown was still the bad guys. Who knew what they were capable of doing?

She gestured to his weapon. "You wouldn't happen to have another one of those, would you?"

He arched an eyebrow. "Do you know how to shoot?"

She lifted her shoulder in a half shrug. "Point and squeeze."

"Right. No, I don't. But you have your Taser, correct?"

"Good point." She dug the small black weapon from her bag and then slipped the strap over her shoulder. She was ready to go.

Despite nerves stretched taut, she and Anthony strolled down the street toward her neighbor's house at a leisurely pace. Hand in hand. Just a young couple out for an evening walk. If only life were that simple. Holding his hand played havoc with her senses, heightening the intensity of the situation.

When they reached Mary and Len's front yard, Anthony pulled her into the inky corner of the Freni property and around the side of the house toward the fenced backyard. After tossing her bag over the fence, he gave her a boost. Heart hammering in her chest, she dropped down on the other side. Thankfully there was no one in sight. She grabbed up her black hobo bag and settled the long strap across her chest and shifted the bag behind her hip so the thing wouldn't restrict her movement or get in her way. A moment later Anthony joined her.

The Freni yard was immaculate, with clipped hedges, potted exotic plants, a lush lawn with a circular patio filled with wood furniture. Interior lights blazed from the bank of windows dominating the back of the house, casting the patio in a soft glow.

In unison they dashed across the large stretch of lawn, just out of reach of the light. Reaching the fence on the opposite side of the yard, Viv almost dropped to her knees with relief. They hadn't been spotted. Again, Anthony helped her up and over the fence, quickly following her into Vivian's backyard.

"No problem." Anthony's voice oozed confidence.

Maybe not for him. She, however, was shaking. "You may be an adrenaline junkie but I'm having a heart attack here."

He touched her shoulder. When he'd held her hand or helped her over the fence, his touch had been all business. Now he was soothing, warm, gentle, reassuring. Tempting.

"Deep breaths."

Easy for him to say. She did as instructed. In—one, two, three. Out—one, two, three. Anthony checked his watch.

"You have an appointment?" she asked.

"Yeah, actually we do."

From her peripheral, she saw a man drop down from the fence next to them. He carried a big, nasty-looking rifle. The strap to a large bag hung across his chest. Her hand holding the Taser rose in a protective gesture. Her startled yelp was cut short by Anthony's hand clamped over her mouth.

"Shh. It's okay," he said.

She peeled his hand away and sucked in air. Stepping closer to Anthony she tried to make out the man's features, but where they stood was too dark.

"Hey, bro, right on time," Anthony whispered to the man shrouded in inky blackness.

"Did you expect anything less?" the man quipped as he withdrew a flashlight from his bag and handed it to Anthony.

Surprise arched through Viv. "Real bro, or 'I'm too cool to use English properly' bro?"

"Vivian Grant, meet Joe Carlucci. My real little brother."

Not so little. Joe stood nearly as tall at Anthony. The darkness hid his face so she couldn't tell if they resembled each other or not. She remembered Anthony mentioning both of his siblings were in law enforcement. "Are you Secret Service too?"

"Nope, ATF," Joe responded, his deep baritone voice similar to his brother's.

"Okay, let's get this party started," Anthony said as he took her by the elbow and led her to the back patio door.

Crime scene tape barred the access to the door.

Dread gripped her. She didn't want to walk back inside the room where Steven had died. But going through the front was out of the question, so she bolstered her courage. The blinking light of the security system caught her attention. "The alarm's on."

"You do know the de-arm code, right?" Joe asked.

"Yes. I'll have about twenty seconds to enter the code on the keypad before the alarm goes off."

Anthony used the van's key to cut through the yellow tape.

"You know how much trouble we're in right now?" Joe stated in a flat voice.

"Hey, you're a federal agent. She's the owner. How much trouble could we get in?

If you're worried, you can arrest me when this over," Anthony shot back.

"Naw. I'll just tell Mom."

Anthony snorted and popped the lock on the slider. The door slid soundlessly open. "Here you go."

Ignoring the musty odor wafting from within the closed-up room, Viv hustled inside and entered the code on the alarm system keypad mounted on the wall. A moment later the red light turned green and the pad chimed indicating the system was disarmed.

Anthony and Joe flipped on the flashlights they carried.

"This way," she said, anxious to find what they came for and get out.

Anthony held her back with a firm grip. He moved in front of her. "You stay between us."

Keeping her gaze straight and not on the chair where she'd last seen Steven's body, she directed the two men out of the study, through the entryway toward the dining room.

"Whoa!" Joe's exclamation brought her up short.

Anthony swung the flashlight in an arc over the formal living room to their right. The place had been ransacked. Her beautiful Queen Anne–style furniture had been destroyed, the cushions ripped apart, the bookcases demolished and the accessories that made the room once so elegant now lay littered on the floor.

Viv's insides clenched. Such a waste. She hated to think what her and Mikey's bedrooms looked like. Those rooms had been their sanctuaries.

"Do you think they found what they were looking for?" Joe asked.

"I doubt it." Viv moved toward the dining room. The intricately carved formal dining set was intact, but the cushions of the chairs had slashes in their seats. Mindless destruction.

She opened the door to a wardrobe. The clothes that had once hung from the rod were lumped on the floor, but thankfully it didn't look like they'd found the rear hidden opening that led to the wall. She felt along the rear wall for the mechanism that would open the back of the wardrobe to reveal the hidden doorway and stairs leading downward.

"Clever," Anthony said.

"This house was built in the twenties during prohibition. At one time there was an illegal distillery down there. Then during the cold war it was refitted to be a fallout shelter. When we bought the house we remodeled and fitted it with a wine rack."

"Cool," Joe said.

"Who knew about this room?" Anthony shined his light down the inky staircase.

Knowing he was thinking about the Wanderer Alert, she said, "Only the contractor, his men and us. We bought this house eight years ago. I don't believe Steven ever brought anyone down here. I sure didn't. Not even the housekeeper."

Anthony found the light switch on the wall inside the opening. "Let me go first."

"Watch your step," she cautioned as she allowed him to enter the passageway. "You'll have to duck. The ceiling's not very high."

They descended the stairs. A bare bulb burned overhead, giving light to the square room. Full, wooden wine racks lined one wall. In the corner was a cold-storage unit filled with champagne and white wine.

"Steven was a wine connoisseur," Viv said, feeling embarrassed by the glut of his collection. She hadn't been down here in years and hadn't realized how much he'd accumulated.

"The safe," Anthony said.

She stepped toward a covered table. "Over here."

Joe helped her remove the many wine goblets sitting on top. She smiled her thanks and got her first real look at him. He did resemble his brother, only Joe's dark hair was longer and more unruly. He had the same strong jaw. His eyes were a lighter shade of brown than Anthony's. He was also armed. A rifle hung over his back and a handgun was stuck in the waistband of his black cargo pants. She didn't want to know what weighted down the pockets.

The show of force unnerved her.

Anthony helped her slide the table aside. She drew back the round area rug to reveal a safe set into the concrete flooring.

"Tell me you can open this," Anthony said, his voice sliding over her as she straightened.

She hadn't realized he'd moved so close. His nearness kindled a warmth deep inside. She wanted to turn into his broad chest and bury her head, pretend none of this was happening.

She didn't.

No amount of wishing would release her from this nightmare. Only the information held inside the safe offered freedom. Not able to find her voice, she nodded.

Reluctantly, she stepped away, pulled off her bag and knelt before the safe. Dredging up the combination from the recesses of her memory, she twisted the dial. The contractor had given her the numbers by mistake. He hadn't known Steven had wanted to keep the safe a secret. But since he wasn't at home that day, she'd been the one to oversee the installation.

Within a moment, she heard the distinct click as the lock tumbled into place. She turned the metal handle and swung the safe's door open.

Anthony knelt beside her, crowding her space, making her acutely aware of him. He aimed the beam of the flashlight on the contents of the safe's two shelves. Several jewelry boxes lay on the top shelf. All the glittery pieces Steven had demanded she wear during public appearances. A diamond-studded tiara from her last pageant win twinkled in the light. She'd wondered where they were, not that she missed them. In fact, seeing the items from her pageant days made her glad she was past that part of her life.

Ignoring the gaudy display, her gaze fell on the stack of file folders. Amid the insurance information, house and tax papers was a file folder labeled *Campaign*.

She opened the file on her lap so Anthony and Joe could see it. Her heart began to hammer against her ribs. "Is this what I think it is?"

"Joe, take a look," Anthony said.

Joe leaned over their shoulders and whistled between his teeth. "What you have here is a ledger of campaign donations."

He pointed to the first column that listed initials next to dollar amounts and then to a second column showing dates and the same dollar amount. "And here is where the donation is reimbursed. Question is, who's doing the reimbursing and who do all the initials belong to?"

Viv's mind reeled. She had no doubt who was doing the reimbursing. One look at the date and the amount and memories shifted, falling into place. She'd noticed several strange withdrawals the one time she'd dared to peek at their bank statement. When she'd questioned Steven, he'd grown angry and demanded she leave the finances to him. He'd threatened to cut her monthly stipend otherwise.

Obviously, Steven had been involved in a straw donor scam. With the news filled lately with the courts revisiting the case against an ex-presidential candidate for this very thing, Viv was familiar with how the scam worked—the illegal practice of using someone else's money to make political contributions in their name and then reimbursing them.

So in essence Steven was funding his own presidential campaign, yet he'd boasted of large backing from both private and corporate funding making it seem that he had a large constituency.

A faint noise raised the hairs on the back of her neck. She grabbed Anthony's arm. "Someone's in the house."

He flipped off the flashlight and searched her face. "You sure?"

"Yes." She'd lived in this house long enough to know every sound, every creak and shift. What she'd heard was someone walking across the dining room. She pointed upward. "The boards squeak."

Joe turned out his flashlight and unscrewed the overhead lightbulb. They hadn't closed the wardrobe door or the door to the staircase behind them. The beam of a flashlight bounced off the wall, giving credence to her words.

Adrenaline jolted Viv to her feet. "This way," she whispered and tugged at Anthony's arm.

"Joe," Anthony called softly.

"Right behind you," he replied.

Viv maneuvered to the wine rack. Feeling along the edge, she found the lip where the rack separated from the wall. "Help me pull this back," she whispered frantically.

In the dark, Anthony's hand slid down her arm to cover her hands. Behind them the flashlights moved down the stairs, bringing danger with the light.

Working together, they tugged on the rack. With a groan of protest the big piece of wood slid away from the wall. Damp air washed over her but didn't cool her panic. The sound of a bottle falling and breaking on the stone floor shattered through the darkness.

Angry shouts of men filled Viv's ears as she slipped through the opening in the wall behind the wine rack. The file folder threatened to slide out of her sweating hand. Behind her, Anthony and Joe pulled the wine rack closed; the sound of wood scraping on concrete echoed off the tunnel walls.

"This way." She ran down the short earthen tunnel supported by thick wooden beam to a metal door. Anthony and Joe were quick on her heels.

Shoving the file into Anthony's hands, she felt along the top of the door until her hand closed over the skeleton key.

At the other end of the tunnel, the wine

rack groaned a protest as their pursuers found their escape route. Lights glinted off the metal door as whoever was behind them tugged the heavy rack open and entered the tunnel. The sharp rap of gunfire exploded around Viv. A man screamed, the sound absorbed by the dirt walls of the tunnel.

Ears ringing, Viv glanced over her shoulder to assure herself Anthony and his brother weren't the one's who'd been hit. They were unharmed and using their bodies as a shield for her. With a renewed sense of urgency, she concentrated on getting the key in the lock. A quick twist and a push sent the metal door swinging wide. A hard body pushed her through the opening and up the short set of steps to the outside patio behind the detached garage.

"This way," Anthony yelled as he propelled her toward the garage's back door.

The house's motion-sensitive outdoor floodlights came on. Viv blinked at the sudden glare.

"Go, go," Joe shouted from behind them. "I've got your six."

More shots were fired. A bullet hit the brick patio. Shards stung Viv's legs through her jeans as she raced with Anthony. At the back door of the garage, Anthony used his elbow to break the window and reached through the opening to unlock the door. They rushed inside. Joe came in after them and hunkered down by the door. He stuck his rifle out the broken window and returned fire.

So much for keeping the neighbors unaware they were here.

"Do you have the keys to either of these cars?" Anthony asked as he pulled her down behind Steven's sports coupe. Next to it sat her luxury sedan.

"Find us a way out, bro," Joe yelled.

"Working on it," Anthony shot back.

"My keys are in my bag," Viv said with a sinking feeling. "Which is back in the wine cellar."

"Great. I led us into a deathtrap."

NINE

Self-disgust pumped through Anthony's veins. The humid July air trapped within the confines of the closed-up garage mingled with the acrid smell of gunpowder, and fear clogged his lungs. Forcing in a breath, he fought frustration and guilt for having put Viv in this situation.

The barrage of gunfire ceased. The sudden eerie silence was somehow more frightening than the chaos of noise and bullets flying. The fear in Vivian's eyes helped him keep his own alarm in check. She needed him to be brave. Pushing aside his doubts and fears of failing her, he touched her cheek, the skin soft beneath the rough pads of his fingertips. "It'll be okay."

"I'm praying so."

"Still clinging, huh?"

"With everything I have."

"Good for you." He wasn't sure he had

enough faith to believe God would help them, but apparently she did.

"Stay put and stay down," he cautioned.

Just because there were no bullets flying now didn't mean a sharpshooter wasn't at the ready to take a well-aimed shot. He started to move away, then hesitated. They could use every bit of help possible. "And keep praying."

She nodded and ducked lower.

In a crouch, he moved to stack up on the right side of the door opposite his brother. He peered out at the empty yard. "Where are they?"

"Can't tell." The harsh lines of concentration on Joe's face were barely discernable in the glow coming from the house's outside floodlights. "They fanned out. We're surrounded. Time to make tracks."

Knowing his brother's aptitude with engines, Anthony gestured with his head toward the two expensive cars parked in the garage. "Can you get one of those babies started?"

Shoving the M16 A1 against Anthony's chest, Joe scoffed. "Like there's any doubt?"

"Go for it, bro." Anthony holstered his SIG and gripped the assault rifle. The weight of the machine in his hand ratcheted up his already heightened adrenaline. For a second he flashed back to his training days at Rowley Training Center located just outside of D.C. He'd thought the police academy had been grueling, but that had been a cakewalk compared to Rowley.

Too bad this wasn't a training exercise.

Staring out at the shadows shifting in the yard, he analyzed the situation. They were trapped within the detached garage, surrounded by assassins out for blood. Whatever information was in that file was worth killing for.

They shouldn't have stopped firing. They'd already shown they weren't concerned with collateral damage. They had to be up to something. He glanced around, trying to put himself into the bad guy's head.

In the distance a siren wailed, drawing closer. The acrid smell of accelerant-laced smoke curled under Anthony's nostrils, alerting him seconds before the west wall of the garage burst into flames.

One question answered. They hoped to burn them out.

"Joe!" Anthony yelled. "Hurry!"

The engine in the big luxury sedan turned over. Joe sat in the driver's seat and flashed the thumbs up sign. Anthony left his post by the door to urge Viv into the backseat. He jumped into the passenger seat.

"You know they're right outside," Joe said evenly.

"Yeah, I know," Anthony replied grimly. To Viv he said, "Down on the floor."

She scrambled off the seat and onto the floorboard. Her hands covered her head.

"To door or not to door?" Joe quipped. Peculiar shadows created by the flames engulfing the garage played across his face.

Not wanting to waste precious seconds waiting for the garage door to rumble open, Anthony said, "Gun it."

Joe flashed a grin as if they were kids playing with Hot Wheels cars. He threw the transmission into Reverse. "Brace yourselves."

He hit the gas. The car shot backward. The wooden garage door barely slowed the sedan's acceleration out of the garage and down the driveway. Armed men dressed in black dove out of the way.

The ping of bullets hitting the metal exterior of the car echoed inside Anthony's head. Viv screamed.

His fear meter shot up. He clamped his jaw tight and hung on.

The front windshield took a hit. A million spidery cracks splintered from a small hole.

The bullet found a home in the backrest of the seat, inches from Anthony.

The old bullet wound in his shoulder ached with memory. He shuddered.

On the narrow residential street, Joe expertly spun the car 180 degrees, narrowly avoiding a parked car, and shifted into Drive. Tires squealed. The back end fishtailed as the car rocketed forward.

Relief wouldn't come until they were far away from there. Anthony kicked the useless front windshield out with his foot. In one huge chunk, the glass slid off the hood and fell to the road. Anthony glanced in the side mirror. So far they weren't being followed.

"We've got to ditch this ride ASAP, bro," Joe said.

"I know. Head to the National Zoo."

"The petting zoo isn't there anymore, Tony," Joe remarked drily.

"I saw a billboard as we drove into the city advertising an evening concert for tonight," Anthony replied.

"All right, then. To the zoo." Joe made a face. "Uh, you'll have to give directions. The zoo isn't a regular haunt of mine when I'm in town."

"Viv?" Anthony looked over his shoulder to the back of the car.

Viv unwound and sat up. She still had the file folder clutched against her chest. Visibly shaken, she placed a hand on Anthony's shoulder. The contact zinged through him, poking holes in his revved-up system.

"Up ahead, take a right on Cathedral and then a left on Connecticut Avenue," she said, her voice shaky. "The entrance isn't far. What about the van?"

"Too risky. We'll get another vehicle in the morning."

Her worried gaze twisted his heart into knots. "We need to check on Mikey."

The knot tightened. Anthony handed her his phone. She dialed and then waited. Her eyebrows drew together in an anxious frown. "Barb's not answering."

Exchanging a troubled glance with his brother, Anthony said, "We'll take the metro and go retrieve him."

Tears welled in Viv's pretty eyes. Her bleak expression tore at Anthony's heart. He wasn't sure risking her life was worth the evidence in her hands. Her quick thinking and bravery had gotten them out of a sticky situation that could have easily been the end of all of them. He respected and admired her more with each passing moment.

Joe motioned to the tactical rifle clutched

in Anthony's hands. He said, "Tear that bad boy down, will ya? Shouldn't be seen out in public."

"Right." Anthony made quick work of dissembling the rifle and stuffed the pieces into Joe's to-go bag.

When they reached the zoo parking lot, Joe slid the sedan into a space between two SUV's.

"Let's move," Anthony said.

They quickly jogged to the metro station entrance, paid the machine for fare tickets and caught the red line to Gallery Place-Chinatown station. There they switched to the green line before departing the subway system at the Columbia Heights station. Anthony kept a hand at the small of Viv's back as they briskly walked the few blocks to Barb's apartment building. He could tell she wanted to run, but the less attention they drew to themselves the better.

The second they entered the foyer, dread slithered up Anthony's spine. "The doorman's not at his post."

"Maybe he's just in the restroom," Viv offered with desperate hope lacing her words.

Exchanging a grim look with Joe, Anthony withdrew his weapon. Viv's eyes widened with panic. He wanted to reassure her that everything was fine. He wanted to believe the doorman had stepped away from his desk and would return momentarily. But his gut said something was wrong.

"Stay behind me," Anthony instructed. "We'll take the stairs. Easier to see an enemy coming and more escape routes."

The stairwell was empty. They proceeded upward, Anthony on point, Viv in the middle and Joe protecting their flank. When they reached the seventh floor, Anthony slowly opened the door. Joe moved past him with a 9 mm Glock in a two-handed grip leading the way.

Viv clutched the back of Anthony's shirt, her terror a palpable thing, fueling his own fear.

"Hall's clear," Joe said.

Anthony knew relief wouldn't come until they had Mikey with them. Taking one of Viv's hands, he led her out of the stairwell and down the hall to Barb's door. His breath stalled for a fraction of a second.

The lock on the door had been busted apart.

The door stood ajar.

Viv let out a small cry of alarm. Anthony immediately gestured for silence. Tears leaked from her eyes. His heart twisted.

Terror invaded his system as violent images of what they might find inside flickered across his mind. He had to protect Viv. He pulled her against him with one arm and nodded to Joe.

Grim-faced, Joe went in leading with his weapon. A moment later he called out, "Clear."

Bracing himself, Anthony led Viv inside, trying to keep her behind him until he could see the damage for himself but she yanked free of his grip and rushed forward only to abruptly halt.

"Oh, no!" Viv sank to her knees, the file folder and its contents spilling onto the carpet.

Anthony took in the scene before him. Horror filled his veins.

Barb Jetton was strapped to a chair with plastic ties; duct tape covered her mouth. Her brown eyes were red and swollen. Blood smeared her chin and spotted her blouse.

Mikey was nowhere in sight. His tattered teddy bear lay facedown on the carpet. Anthony's stomach dropped. His worst nightmare had become a reality. Fear splintered through him. Failure ripped his heart to shreds.

Joe knelt beside Barb. "I'm going to take the tape off. This might hurt."

Barb nodded. Joe grasped an edge of the tape and tore it free. Barb cried out. "Three men broke in. They took…" A sob escaped. "They took Mikey."

Viv let out a guttural groan like a wounded animal. Her whole body rocked as tears fell down her cheeks. "No, no, no."

Joe cut the ties binding Barb to the chair and helped her to stand. "Are you hurt?"

"Just a busted lip."

"You need ice," Joe said.

Barb shook her head. "I'm okay. We have to find Mikey."

Hanging on to his composure by a thread, Anthony scrubbed a hand over his face. Anguish threatened to drive him to his knees. He fought to remain calm. Giving in to his own horror wouldn't help Viv. Wouldn't save Mikey. "Did you recognize any of the men?"

Barb grimaced. "They wore masks. But Mikey grew really agitated when the one in charge barked out orders, kind of like he recognized the voice."

The significance of that information jolted through Anthony.

Viv's gaze snapped to his. "Steven's killer!"

At a loss for words, Anthony nodded. Panic and dread scurried along his veins like a million tiny ants. A shiver of pure terror prickled his flesh.

"I should never have left him."

Viv's desolate tone slammed into Anthony, knocking him back a step. Self-reproach tore at his insides, slicing what little confidence he'd managed to build up over the past few days to bits of nothingness.

He should have known better than to think he could protect anyone.

Mikey was gone. Viv felt as if her heart had been ripped from her chest, leaving a big gaping hole of loss and desolation. Kidnapped by a murderer. She had no way of knowing if the killer had already ended her son's life. She shivered with a mixture of shock and fear and guilt.

Mikey.

How could she go on without him? He was her reason for living. The only thing that mattered. She squeezed her eyes shut, blocking out the blame rising in her soul. She wanted to rail at Anthony, at herself. At God.

As quickly as that last thought formed, she rejected it. She wouldn't let a life emergency, a life tragedy, create a crisis of faith within her. This was her fault. Not God's.

She should never have let Mikey out of

her sight. If she'd listened to Anthony's concerns and not demanded they return to D.C., she and Mikey would be safe right now in Boston.

A deep soul-searing ache wrenched the breath from Viv. She shuddered as she tried to contain the welling grief.

She was the one to blame for Mikey's disappearance. She'd been so stupid. Selfish.

There was no place safe.

Barb fell to her knees at her side. "Viv, I'm so sorry."

Viv clung to her friend. "Not your fault. We shouldn't have brought Mikey here. This was my decision. My mistake."

One which had most likely cost her son his life.

Strong hands gently pulled her to her feet. Anthony lifted her chin with a shaky hand to meet his gaze. She saw the same wretchedness she felt reflected in his dark irises. "This isn't your fault, it's mine. I've failed you."

Horrible pain consumed her. She trembled. "No. You said it was too dangerous coming back to D.C. I shouldn't have been so selfish. I wanted to clear my name. I—"

He placed the pad of his finger to her lips. "Shh. No. Don't blame yourself. It was my job to protect you. I failed. I'm—"

The shrill ring of a phone cut him off.

Barb pointed to the dining table. A cell phone lay in the middle. It vibrated as it rang. "That's not mine."

Viv's heart pitched. The kidnappers calling? That would mean Mikey was still alive.

She curbed the impulse to make a grab for it as Anthony picked up a cloth napkin and reached for the phone. Carefully, using the cloth to avoid smearing any prints, he answered. "Yes."

Tension constricted Viv's breath. Time seemed to stand still. Anthony listened to the person on the other line, his face giving away nothing.

"I want proof of life," Anthony said.

Viv's heart froze. Hope flared.

Mikey's shrill, unmistakable cry emanated from the phone.

A whimper filled the room and Viv realized it came from her. Relief blasted over her, making her breath stall. *Her son was alive!* A hysterical burst of happy relief threatened to escape.

But for how long?

Anthony's eyes closed and his head hung forward for a second. When he lifted his head and opened his eyes, hard determination shone bright. "Fine." He hung up.

Rushing to his side, Viv asked, "What? What do they want?"

His arm slid around her, offering her comfort she desperately needed. She clung to him. His support, his caring filled all the damaged places inside. He would make this right. *Please, dear God, let him make it right.*

"They want the file folder," Anthony said. "You and I are to meet them at the northwest corner of the Washington Monument at sunrise."

One glance at the clock said they had less than a half hour. Viv tried to picture the area, but her mind was too freaked, her guilt too strong, to make any coherent images. All she wanted was to have Mikey back in her arms.

All business now, Anthony gestured to the scattered papers on the floor. "Viv, can you gather those up? Ms. Jetton, do you have a fax machine?"

Barb gestured to her computer station in the corner of the living room. "Yes. Over there."

Thankful for something to distract her, Viv scooped up the papers and arranged them back in the file folder. Her gaze scanned the pages. All the numbers, so much money changing hands. All those initials. Was one of these people behind Steven's death? Did one of these people have Mikey now? White-hot anger crawled over her fear. She wanted to make the person responsible hurt in the worst way.

"Where do you want to send them?" she asked Anthony.

"To Trent." Anthony fished a business card out of his pocket. "The fax number is on there. They'll know what to do with this information."

Viv followed Barb to the computer. Within a few seconds they had the pages feeding through the copier and transmitting through the wireless cable to Trent Associates.

"We're going to need help, Tony," Joe stated.

Viv glanced over to see Anthony's reaction.

His expression was grim as he ran a hand through his hair. "I know. Trent will provide backup."

"No time, bro. We need to reach out to your pals in the Secret Service."

Anthony flinched liked he'd been hit. He shook his head. "No can do. I'm not sure whoever is orchestrating this operation hasn't compromised the Service the way they have the FBI."

Viv nodded her agreement. She still had trouble believing how deep and wide this thing went. And they didn't even know who was behind Steven's death, the straw donor scam or Mikey's kidnapping.

Joe made a derisive face. "You're going to have to take the risk. We need to set a perimeter around the monument and take these guys down. And we need to make sure if this turns ugly, innocent bystanders aren't caught in the crossfire."

Anthony blew out a breath. "I'll make the call."

He took out his cell phone and moved a couple of steps away. Viv could appreciate his ability to concede to the wisdom of others. Unfortunately, conceding to her wisdom regarding coming to D.C. had been a mistake. Had he made a similar mistake that had cost his last assignment his life?

The thought rocked her confidence in her bodyguard. And he'd become so much more… She pushed that knowledge away.

The few facts she knew about the event that had changed his life didn't lead her to think he'd made some kind of mistake, yet he'd been let go from the Secret Service. That had to mean something.

Barb wrapped her arm around Viv's waist. "We'll get him back," she said.

Viv leaned into her. "I pray so."

"Ms. Jetton, do you have a car we can use?" Joe asked.

"I do. I'll get my keys. They're in my purse in the bedroom." She hurried away, disappearing down the hall.

Viv wrapped her arms around her middle in an attempt to keep herself together. Giving in to the myriad emotions ricocheting through her wouldn't do her son any good. Her gaze moved to Anthony. He had his back to them. She could hear the low rumble of his voice as he talked. She loved the soothing tones.

"We'll get your son back."

She turned to stare at Joe. His dark eyes, so similar in expression and shape to his brother's, regarded her with compassion and intelligence. Though Joe's eyes were dark, they were more chocolate than Anthony's, and the angles and planes of his face weren't nearly as finely etched. But there was the same determined jut to Joe's chin as Anthony's.

"I want to believe so." Her lower lip quivered as doubts assaulted her.

"My brother is the best at what he does," Joe said with obvious pride in his voice.

"Then why'd the Secret Service let him go?"

Creases formed between Joe's brows. "They didn't let him go. He quit."

That news set her back on her heels. "Oh. I assumed after the assassination he'd been fired."

Joe let out a snort. "No. In fact, they'd take him back in a heartbeat. He's the only one who thinks he failed. He did his job. There's only so much a person can do in some situations. Even if they do have a hero complex."

"Your brother doesn't have a hero complex." At least she hadn't seen it. He'd been gracious and unassuming this whole time, never showing any sign of arrogance that would lead her to believe he carried such a lofty view of himself.

Joe's mouth quirked. "Yeah, well, to me and my sis, he's everything we want to be."

The apparent love and pride in Joe's voice touched Viv, reminding her of all the reasons she'd come to trust Anthony. His compassion toward her son, his ability to react quickly under pressure and his strength of character. She felt a little ashamed to have let any doubts in.

Barb returned from her room with car keys in hand. She'd changed clothes, putting on dark slacks, a green shirt that accentuated her red hair, and tennis shoes. She'd washed the blood away from her oval-shaped face and her brown eyes were clear with determination. She held out the keys to Joe.

As his hand wrapped around the small, fuzzy rabbit-foot keychain, she held on. "I'm coming with you."

Joe frowned. "No way. Too dangerous. You'll just be a liability."

Barb hiked up an eyebrow. "Excuse me. I can help."

His lip curled. "I beg to differ."

"Beg all you want. But I'm coming." She yanked the keys back and held on to them.

Joe narrowed his gaze. "You're one stubborn woman."

Barb lifted her chin. "I work with more difficult children than you. I have to be stubborn."

Viv watched the exchange with interest, grateful for the distraction. When Joe's sudden grin brought a blush to Barb's cheeks, Viv couldn't stop a slight smile from forming. She doubted either of the two was aware of the sparks they were setting off, like sparklers on the Fourth of July.

Anthony clicked off from his phone call and strode to her side. "A detail will meet us at the site in ten. We've got to roll. Viv, you stay with Barb."

"No!" she protested. "No way am I staying behind. The kidnappers said I was to come with you."

He frowned. "This might get messy. I don't want you to get hurt."

"Too late for that. Every second Mikey is out there I hurt. You're going to need me and Barb when you find Mikey."

Indecision crossed his features. "Viv."

"I know you know what you're doing. I'll do exactly what you tell me to."

Acceptance softened the tight line of his mouth. He touched her cheek. "Okay."

With a smirk directed at Joe, Barb flounced out the apartment door ahead of him.

Joe gave his brother a tortured look as they followed Barb to the stairwell. "Really? You just had to agree to her coming, didn't you?"

"Can the complaints, bro," Anthony said. "Viv and Mikey will need her."

Viv gripped the file folder tightly to her chest. She sent up a silent prayer that the exchange would go off without gunfire or bloodshed. That her son would be unhurt.

* * *

The first of the sun's soft rays pinkened the distant horizon. The sound of fifty American flags flapping in the wind echoed the chaos going on inside of Anthony. Fear and anger at himself warred for dominance in his psyche. Huge floodlights chased away the remnants of night as he walked a short path on the concrete platform surrounding the monolithic Washington Monument's northwest corner. He held the file folder in one hand and the cell phone in the other as instructed.

A forensic examiner had dusted the cell phone for fingerprints as soon as Anthony had arrived on scene. Unfortunately, there were none. The phone was a prepaid, bought at a convenience store that made tracing the purchaser next to impossible. Given time they could find the store and view the security video footage and hope to get an ID—that is if the store had working security cameras. But there was no time.

The incoming call from the kidnapper had also been from a prepaid phone that was now out of service. Whoever was behind this knew what they were doing. Most likely professionals.

Viv stood a little distance away, quiet and obviously scared. She twisted her finger much the way her son did when upset. A learned behavior or an inherited one?

Every time Anthony caught a glimpse of her, his heart contracted. He didn't want to fail her.

You already did, a voice inside his head mocked.

The knowledge soured his stomach. Blame raised its ugly head. Anthony was tempted to accuse God of failing Viv, of not answering her prayers. But the accusation wouldn't come.

Because the responsibility for Viv and Mikey's safety lay on his shoulders. He'd been charged with their protection. Everyone expected him to keep them from harm.

He vowed to do anything and everything he could to get Mikey back.

Unseen agents encircled the area both to protect and to apprehend, and intermingled with the early-morning crowd of tourists visiting the national attraction. There hadn't been time for more sophisticated surveillance. A microphone was hidden in the lapel of Anthony's jacket and an earbud let him communicate with the special agent in charge of this quickly-put-together undertaking.

His brother was close; he and the feisty Barb Jetton were pretending to be tourists.

Knowing Joe had his back made Anthony feel better since he wasn't sure that he could completely trust the government agents. He hated doubting the men and women he'd once served with. Hated thinking that anyone of them could be dirty.

But to be on the safe side, he and Joe had agreed it would be better if the agents did not know of Joe's presence or that a copy of the file had been faxed to Trent Associates. The backup set of documents kept Anthony's tension from becoming overwhelming. Even if the handoff went bust, they still had their evidence.

The cell in his hand vibrated. *Here we go.* Gut clenching, Anthony pressed the talk button. "Yes?"

"Listen carefully," said the same altered voice that had called earlier. "Take out the earbud and ditch the microphone."

Anger fisted in his chest. He'd been right. The bad guys had infiltrated the Secret Service. "I don't know what you're talking about."

The man scoffed. "Don't underestimate me. I know every move you make. Cooperate or you'll never see the boy alive again."

Frustration pounded at Anthony's temple. In his other ear, Special Agent Gorman said,

"We heard. I'll take care of it on this end. You follow the plan."

The man on the phone said, "Are you really going to let this boy die?"

Every fiber of Anthony's being said to stick with the plan, to trust the men and women he'd served with. But someone had compromised the situation. He had to go against all his training and do what needed to be done to save Mikey. He took the earbud out, dropping it on the ground. Next he removed the microphone and tossed it aside.

"I did as you asked. Now what?"

"You and the widow Grant need to make your way to the castle on the National Mall. Make sure you're not followed or this boy's death is on your head."

The line went dead.

A boulder-size knot lodged itself in Anthony's throat. Nearly choking on fear and adrenaline, he slipped the phone into his jacket pocket before closing the distance between him and Viv. He snagged her by the elbow and drew her to his side. "We've got a problem."

"What happened? What did the kidnapper say?" she asked.

"They know the agents are here."

"How?" Her eyes widened when understanding hit. "They have someone in the agency, don't they? Just like with the FBI. Now what?" The color drained from her face. Her short-cropped dark hair fluttered in the breeze. "How do we get Mikey back now?" she asked in a strangled voice.

"They want us to walk to the Smithsonian Castle. But first we have to ditch the service detail." He glanced around, looking for the best possible escape route. He saw a cluster of tourists gathering near the walkway. A tour guide held up a flag. Anthony spun Viv around so she was facing the walkway. "See the tour group over there?"

"Yes."

Though it went against every tenant of protection service, they had to separate. "When I give you the word, you're going to hustle over and join them. Worm your way to the middle and stay with them. Make your way to the Mall. I'll meet you in front of the castle."

She glanced over her shoulder at him. "What are you going to do?"

"I'm going to take a hike around the monument, let Joe know what's up and hopefully confuse the agents."

Turning to face him, she said, "I don't think we should separate."

Cupping her cheek, he bent close, stopping a breath from her lips. "Trust me?"

She blinked. Swallowed. Nodded. Her hand clutched the front of his shirt and tugged him all the way. Their lips met. The contact was full of fear, hope and something else. Something he had no intention of examining. He drew back. "We'll get him back and get through this alive."

"I'm praying so."

"How can you still believe that God cares after all that's happened?"

A crease formed between her delicate eyebrows. "I can't let circumstances dictate my faith in God."

Her conviction in the face of such uncertainty and peril baffled and amazed him. And stirred something deep inside of him, making him want to believe that God would come through for them.

He took half the contents of the file folder and shoved them into her hand. "This way, they have to have both of us if they want the complete file."

She held the papers against her chest, the stark white a contrast to the bright red shirt she wore. He spun her around again and gave her a gentle push. Visibly squaring her shoulders, she took off, darting through the crowds toward the tour group as the mass of tourists started to move away from the monument.

Pride filled Anthony's chest. All his pre-conceived notions of the pretentious beauty queen had long since bitten the dust. In their place was respect for her strength of character and courage in the face of hardship, and affection for her indomitable spirit and quick intelligence.

If he weren't careful he'd find himself falling in love with her. And that was something he could not allow. There was an unwritten rule among those who protected others: *you do not fall in love with your protectee!*

He forced himself to move, to turn away and briskly head in the opposite direction.

Spotting Joe and Barb off to the side near one of the many plaques that gave insight into the monument's history, Anthony veered closer, then purposefully let the file folder fall. The remaining papers scattered. Joe and Barb immediately bent to help pick up the mess.

"What gives?" Joe asked.

"Mole. Head to the Smithsonian Castle."

He took the pages Joe and Barb had collected with a nod of thanks and hurried away. The keys to Barb's Volvo jingled in his pocket. Deciding to take the car, he jogged for the parking lot where they'd left the vehicle.

"Hey! Carlucci! Stop!"

Anthony ignored the shouted command.

The sound of running feet sent his heart rate into overdrive.

Mikey's life rested on ditching the security Anthony had arranged.

Those guys were good. The best, actually.

He hoped he could make it. If he didn't, he'd fail all over again.

TEN

Streetlamps clicked off as the sun rose higher in the early-morning sky. Trying to control her racing pulse, Viv shuffled along with the tour group crossing Fourteenth Street and entered the National Mall park. Her half of the file was still pressed against her chest like a shield. According to Anthony, these papers would keep her alive. But every time someone bumped or jostled into her, she flinched, half expecting the bad guys to grab her.

Please, Lord, give me strength.

She had to be strong. For Mikey. For Anthony.

Adjusting her grip on the papers, she followed the group along the dirt track rimming the sparse lawn of the mall where tents and vendors were setting up in preparation for tomorrow's Fourth of July celebration.

The tour guide pointed to the left, introducing the group to the first of the Smithsonian museums across the street from the park. Viv stayed smack dab in the middle of the crowd until they were directly in front of the Smithsonian's castle, then she peeled away as discreetly as she could.

The red sandstone landmark indeed resembled a twelfth-century castle. She'd always liked coming here before. She'd brought Mikey once last summer. He'd been fascinated with the tactile map of all the Washington monuments and the "touch screen" programs in various languages. Her stomach knotted. Would she have a chance to bring Mikey back here?

With concerted effort she pushed her fear to the far recesses of her mind and hustled across Jefferson Drive. She hurried up the front steps to the entrance. The doors were locked. The museum wouldn't open for another couple of hours.

The entryway left her exposed. Unease trickled through her veins. She looked around, hoping to find some inconspicuous place to wait for Anthony. From her left, the shadows shifted and a man materialized from behind one of the entrance's arched pillars.

The flight response jolted through her system. She spun around intending to retreat back the way she'd come when a strong hand closed over her wrist, stopping her forward progress with an abrupt jerk. She drew in a breath to scream.

"Viv, it's me."

Instantly, she recognized Anthony's voice. Relief sluiced through her body, ridding her of the sudden panic.

But not the fear.

Fear seemed to have taken up permanent residence within her.

She put a hand over her racing heart. "How did you get here so fast?"

"I drove the Volvo. It's parked on the street. I called Joe and let him know where to find it," he answered, drawing her close. "Didn't mean to scare you."

She leaned against him, needing his solid strength. She was so grateful she didn't have to go through this alone. "Have they called?"

"No. We should wait out on the sidewalk where we can be seen."

Though reluctant to leave the shelter of his arms, she nodded and stepped away. She trusted him to know what was best for her and Mikey. Anthony grasped her hand. She held on tight as they descended the front stairs to the sidewalk. Almost immediately, the cell phone in Anthony's jacket pocket trilled.

Dropping her hand, he fished the phone out and answered. "Yes."

As he listened, he spun around so that he was facing east. He seemed to be searching for something. Or maybe it was just her imagination and hopeful thinking. She wanted to hold her son, to wrap her arms around him and make him feel as secure as Anthony had made her feel moments ago.

At the far end of the park, sunlight glinted off the U.S. Capitol building. Anxiousness made her antsy. If only she could hear what was being said, too! She bounced on the balls of her feet.

The second Anthony ended the call, she pounced. "Where's my son? Is he still okay? Where did they take him?"

He held up a hand and she relented. "He's down the street in a parked SUV. We're to give the file to the driver in exchange for Mikey."

She shoved her half of the papers she held at his chest. "Then let's go." She took a step but Anthony caught her by the waist.

"Wait. It could be a trap."

Impatience pounded in her veins. She struggled free. "I don't care. I want my son."

Placing a strong hand on one of her shoulders, he forced her to face him. "You do exactly as I say when I say it. Any hesitation could cost you or Mikey your lives. Got it?"

"Yes." Frustration welled up inside of her, but she knew he was right. If not for her impatience and stubbornness before, they'd still have Mikey with them. "In spades."

He released her with a nod and put the file inside his coat before placing his arm around her waist. At any other time, she'd relish the gesture. Even hope that his closeness meant he cared for her with romantic intent. But she knew romance wasn't motivating his touch. He wanted to keep her close to protect her, as he'd been *hired* to do.

He urged her to walk at a brisk pace. Viv would have preferred to run, anything to reach Mikey faster, but she knew they couldn't draw any more attention to themselves. When they reached the corner of Jefferson Drive and Fourth Street, Anthony steered her across the road and stopped her five feet away from a big, black SUV.

The same sort of SUV the two FBI agents, Jones and Thompson, had put her and Mikey in after Steven's death. She shuddered at the memory.

The driver's-side door opened and a man slid out. He was tall, with a closely shaved head and big muscles beneath a black T-shirt.

He looked like some covert operative from a movie. Without a word, he opened the back passenger door.

Mikey lay across the backseat.

Still and quiet.

Viv's heart lurched and took her body with it. She would make every single one of them pay.

Anthony snagged her around the waist and held her tight, her back against his unyielding chest, as a mother's fury raged within her. She pushed at his arm, wanting to go to her son.

The man shut the door. "The file?"

With one arm snaked around Viv's waist holding her in place, Anthony handed over the folder. "This ends it, right?"

"This is all of it?"

Anthony nodded.

The man flipped the file open and perused the content. "How do we know you didn't make a copy?"

"You don't. Call it insurance," Anthony shot back.

Snapping the folder shut, the man turned on his heel and headed down the street in the opposite direction.

Not able to stand another moment away

from her son, Viv clawed at Anthony's arm. "Let go."

He relented. She broke free and rushed to the vehicle. She yanked open the door and scrambled onto the seat next to Mikey. She checked his pulse and felt a strong beat beneath her fingertips. "Thank You, Jesus."

Gathering him in her arms, she smoothed a hand over his cheek. He felt cool to her touch. "Mikey, oh, honey. Wake up!"

Anthony slid into the driver's seat. He reached for the keys in the ignition. He paused. Swiftly, he pulled his hand away and twisted on the seat to look back at her. The expression of sheer terror on his face shot her fear meter through the roof.

"Get out! Get out now!"

She didn't hesitate. She yanked on the door handle and flung the door wide as she scuttled off the seat, landing on her feet. She reached in to pull Mikey out. He awakened with a jerk and batted at her hands. Anthony joined her and together they managed to get a firm grasp on him and drag him out of the vehicle.

Anthony scooped Mikey up. "Run! Go, go!"

They'd barely put two car lengths between them and the SUV before an explosion ripped through the air behind them. Nearby pedestrians screamed.

The concussion drove Viv to her hands and knees. She cried out at the bone-jarring impact. Her teeth snapped together, sending waves of pain through her head. Debris pelted her in a stinging rain and heat singed her skin. Her breath caught and held in her chest. The ringing in her ears muted the cacophony of noise from car alarms disturbed by the blast and the shouts from pedestrians. Acrid smoke filled the air and burned her lungs.

Frantic, she blinked back tears, her gaze wildly searching for Mikey and Anthony.

She found them a few feet away. She breathed out a moan of relief and pain. Anthony's still body pinned a screaming, struggling Mikey to the ground. He seemed unscathed but scared as he flailed unsuccessfully, trying to get himself out from beneath the big body on top of him.

Compelled by an urgency she didn't understand, she crawled on all fours to Anthony's side. "It's okay, baby. I'm here," she murmured to Mikey to calm him as she touched Anthony's cheek.

Blood from a gash on his forehead marred his handsome face. She laid her fingers against the side of his neck. She could barely detect a pulse. But it was there.

"Anthony! Wake up," she uttered low in her throat as she tried to roll him off her son.

Feet pounded on the sidewalk, jerking her attention toward the people rushing up. She blinked with relief. Joe and Barb skidded to a halt beside her. Joe immediately eased Anthony off Mikey and rolled him onto his back.

Seeing Barb working to calm Mikey freed Viv to put her energy into her concern for Anthony. She sent up a silent plea. *Lord, please, let him be all right.*

"Did he rag doll?" he asked in a low, grim tone.

"What? I have no idea what that means."

"Did the blast throw him through the air with his arms, legs, neck going every which way like a rag doll before he hit the ground?"

Neck? Joe was worried Anthony had a broken neck. Viv pushed down the panic rising up her own neck and answered, "I don't think so. No. No, he still had Mikey in his arms."

"Okay. Outstanding." Joe checked his brother's pulse. "Thready."

Not sure if that was good or not, Viv placed her hand over Anthony's. "What can I do to help?"

"We've got to get out of here." Joe got behind Anthony and slipped his arms beneath his. "We found the Volvo. It's right here."

"Shouldn't we stay and tell the authorities what's happening?" Barb asked.

Joe shook his head and jerked an elbow toward the twisted, smoldering bumper dangling from the lower branches of a nearby cherry tree. "Not sure who to trust at this point. We need to get somewhere safe to regroup."

The information sank to the pit of Viv's stomach like a chunk of SUV. Corruption of any kind was horrible but when it was within the very framework of those who were supposed to be trustworthy it sickened her. "We need to take your brother to the hospital. We can 'regroup' there."

Concern flashed in Joe's eyes. "You're right." Hoisting Anthony up, he said to Viv, "Get his feet."

She grabbed Anthony by the ankles. He moaned as they lifted him off the ground. Viv took that as a good sign even though his eyes stayed closed. Staggering under his weight, she helped carry him to the Volvo which Joe had double-parked a few feet away.

They placed him in the front seat and buckled him in, Viv slid onto the backseat beside Barb and Mikey. Just as the street filled with emergency vehicles, Joe hit the gas, made a U-turn and headed away from the scene of the burning SUV.

Ten minutes later, Joe parked in the emergency bay of Howard University Hospital. The red letters over the door were lit up. Sunlight reflected off the many rectangular windows of the brick building. A uniformed guard sauntered over as Joe climbed out.

"You can't park here," the guard said.

"I'll move it," Joe barked. "But first I've got to get my brother inside."

Viv jumped out and ran around to the front passenger side to help Joe with Anthony.

The guard waved a white-garbed orderly over. The orderly, a young man with round glasses that reminded Viv of a cartoon character, took one look at Anthony and hurried away. He returned moments later with another attendant and a gurney. Viv moved out of the way so the hospital personnel could move Anthony from the car to the gurney.

Anthony's eyelids fluttered then opened as the orderly secured him to the bed.

Tears of relief clogged Viv's throat. She smoothed a hand over Anthony's cheek, the stubble of his beard gently scratching her palm.

Confusion filled his dark eyes; a flash of panic flared them wide. "Mikey?"

Thankful he was awake and lucid, she sought to reassure him. "He's fine. You protected him from the explosion."

Relief softened his gaze. "Good to know." He frowned. "Where are we?"

"Hospital," Viv answered. "You took a nasty hit to your head."

His mouth quirked. "I've got a hard head."

She felt the tug of an answering smile. "Yes, you do. But you still need to be checked by a doctor."

He nodded and closed his eyes again. She was falling for him. Falling hard. There was so much about Anthony Carlucci that drew her in. His honor, his integrity. The way he made her feel beautiful on the inside as well as the outside without any strings attached. The way he risked his life for her and Mikey.

Logic told her these feelings were born of the stress and intensity of coming so close to dying. More than once. But her heart didn't agree. Her heart insisted the tender emotions bubbling deep inside were real and true and lasting. The conflict going on inside stymied her.

"Viv," Anthony said, his voice wobbly.

She took his hand. "I'll be right here. You let them take care of you."

He gave her hand a squeeze before his gaze shot to his brother. "Joe, keep them safe."

Viv could see that Joe wanted to go with his brother. But then his expression set in determined lines. "Will do."

The orderly wheeled Anthony away and disappeared inside the emergency-room doors.

Mikey moved to stand in front of Viv. She placed a hand on his shoulder.

Barb put an arm around Viv's shoulders. "He'll be fine. They'll stitch him up and he'll be good as new."

"I know." But seeing him laid low twisted her up inside. The memory of seeing the scar from the bullet that had ripped through his flesh to kill another slammed through her mind. It was his job to take risks, to put himself in danger for others. For her and Mikey.

His job required he put his life on the line. As he had with the Secret Service and now with her and Mikey. He'd do the same for the next client. And one of these days he wouldn't get so lucky. He could be critically, *fatally* injured.

A whole new kind of fear burned the back of her throat.

No way could she allow herself to fall completely in love with him. She wasn't strong enough. Not when there was a good chance she could lose him.

Anthony sat on the edge of the hospital bed in an exam room. Using a handheld mirror, he stared at the stitches in his head. "Nice job, Doc."

The younger man grinned, his white teeth gleaming bright against his dark complexion. "Now, Mr. Smith, you shouldn't drive or operate any heavy machinery for at least twenty-four hours. If you experience any blurred vision, dizziness, nausea, vomiting or confusion, you need to return right away. I would also recommend you follow up with your regular doctor in a day or so. The stitches will dissolve in about a week's time. If there is any redness, swelling or weeping from the wound, come back in."

Anxious to see Viv and Mikey, to double-check they were safe, Anthony stood. For a moment the world wavered, then righted itself.

Even though his head pounded, he'd refused pain medicine. He needed to stay alert. While he trusted Joe with his life, Anthony needed to find a better way of protecting Viv and her son. He'd let danger get too close. He wouldn't fail to keep them safe, even if that meant letting someone else from Trent take over. "I'll be fine, Doc. Thanks for patching me up. Can I go?"

"Yes, I signed your discharge papers."

Anthony found his way to the waiting area where his brother, Barb, Viv and Mikey occupied seats against the far wall. Joe stood guard, his dark expression clearly intimidating the few other people anxiously awaiting their loved ones.

His gut tightened. It wasn't safe for them to be so visible. He needed to get them out of there to somewhere safe.

Anthony's gaze arrowed straight to Viv. She sat on one of the hard plastic chairs with her back to the wall, her son on her lap. Her drawn expression pulled at his heart. The sharp longing to gather her close stabbed him. He shifted his gaze away to the child sitting on her lap. Mikey clutched his bear to his chest, his sweet young face looking lost. Affection and empathy unfurled and spread through Anthony.

Seeing them both safe eased the constriction in his chest, allowing him to take a full breath. They'd come close to dying tonight. He wasn't going to let that happen again.

Viv's gaze met his. Her whole face lit up. She put Mikey in the empty chair next to her and rushed to meet Anthony in the middle of the room. Anthony's heart did a flip-flop. He absorbed her quick hug, allowing her curves to mold against him. For a brief second, he closed his eyes and savored having her close. But giving in to his growing attachment and affection wasn't going to keep her or Mikey safe.

Action would.

He reluctantly set her away from himself so he could think. Driving to Boston now was out of the question. Too many opportunities for disaster. Even if Trent sent a new protection detail, they wouldn't arrive for hours.

Anthony had to find a safe haven for Viv and Mikey now. Someplace close. They needed a new plan. Thankfully, they weren't alone.

"Joe, you have any pull in the Department of Justice?"

His little brother eyed him curiously. "I know the Assistant Attorney General. What do you have in mind?"

He stared at the woman and boy who had wormed their way into his heart. He wanted them to be able to live their lives in peace, not on the run and in fear. "Hopefully a way to clear Viv's name and bring down whomever is behind the threat to her and Mikey's lives."

Joe grinned. "Ah, a family hunting trip."

Viv sat in the middle of the backseat of the Volvo. A headache throbbed behind her eyes. Mikey had insisted on sitting by the window, so she rolled it down a crack. The fresh air was a welcome relief from the lingering scent of smoke on their clothes. Mikey pressed his nose against the glass and watched the passing scenery as Joe drove them through the bustling city.

Barb sat on Viv's other side. She'd insisted on accompanying them rather than finding somewhere to stay until this nightmare was over. Viv was grateful for Barb's friendship. Having a close woman friend was something decidedly lacking before in Viv's life.

Anthony sat in the front passenger seat next to Joe who was driving. The bandage covering Anthony's head wound was a stark reminder of how easily the morning's events could have taken a tragic turn for the worse.

Viv bit her lip with misgivings after hearing Anthony's idea of contacting the AAG. "How can you be sure the DOJ hasn't been compromised?"

Anthony looked to his brother for the answer.

"I can personally vouch for Kevin Jacobs. He's as solid a citizen as they come." Joe's voice oozed with confidence as he met her gaze through the rearview mirror.

Anthony reached across the center console to take her hand. "Trust me. This is the best way to resolve this. James Trent is faxing over a copy of the file at this moment."

He'd called Trent headquarters before they'd left the hospital. She'd assumed he was requesting more bodyguards or a helicopter to spirit them away or something as equally cloak-and-daggerish. Contacting the DOJ hadn't occurred to her.

"The AAG can place you and Mikey in a safe house while he investigates the straw donor scam and tracks down the people involved."

Anthony's plan made sense on so many levels. By going to the DOJ and relinquishing her safety to the AAG, Anthony would be out of danger. Relief born of her desire to protect him infused her words. "I think that's a brilliant idea then."

He'd be safe.

Until his next assignment.

That thought dampened her enthusiasm for the plan. But at least he wouldn't risk being hurt again while protecting her and Mikey. A burden she didn't want to shoulder any longer.

For some reason Anthony's expression darkened. His gaze shuttered closed. "I'm glad you approve."

His tone was so terse that if she weren't watching the words come out of his mouth, she wouldn't have recognized his voice.

He released her hand and turned toward the front window.

"Air! Want air."

Mikey's insistent demand drew her attention. She was too tired and upset to fight him. She rolled the window all the way down. Mikey stuck his head out.

"Hang on!" Joe shouted, startling Viv out of her thoughts.

The sudden deceleration as Joe slammed on the brakes sent Viv's heart rate galloping. The seat belt locked, painfully biting into her flesh as it stopped her forward momentum. Mikey let out a strangled "ack" as his belt caught, too. The car skidded to halt. A black SUV blocked their path. The door to the vehicle flung open and masked armed men poured out.

Terror jackknifed through Viv. She grabbed for Mikey, trying to cover him.

"Get down!" Anthony's battle-honed cry overlapped with a barrage of gunfire hitting the car.

Barb screamed. Viv fumbled with the seat belt latches. Free, she dove to the floor with Mikey, covering their heads.

Mikey grew agitated by the noise and chaos. Viv struggled to control her fear. She had to shield Mikey. His high-pitched shrieks filled the inside of the car. His hands flapped like wings of a bird.

"Barb, help me get Mikey between us." Frantically Viv reached to pull Mikey past her across the floorboard toward Barb's waiting hands just as he yanked on the door handle. The door popped open.

"No!" Viv held on to his thin body. He kicked, his heel connecting with her abdomen and knocking the wind from her.

He twisted his thin frame out of her grasp. As quick as lightning, he slipped out of the car and ran down the street. Ignoring the dangerous gunfire, Viv scrambled out of the car. Her only thought was to get to Mikey.

"Vivian! No!"

She glanced briefly back in the direction of Anthony's yell. He and Joe were pinned down. There was no way they could help her and Mikey. She had to do this alone. She ran after her son.

The midmorning heat and humidity was oppressive, making her breathing labored. Bullets hit the pavement inches from her feet. Dread tightened her shoulders. The real possibility that any moment a bullet would slam into her almost made her falter, but she kept her gaze fixated on Mikey. Another big black vehicle barreled out from a side street and screeched to a halt, blocking their way. Two more masked armed men jumped out, their weapons raised.

Viv's heart stuttered as fresh fear surged, propelling her feet to move faster. But Mikey stayed just out of reach. Sirens of approaching help added to the chaos.

"Grab the kid!" came a shouted command from inside the vehicle.

A big, muscled man, dressed all in black and wearing a mask, easily snagged Mikey. He turned to carry him to the SUV. Stark terror struck Viv. She couldn't let them take her son again.

She jumped on his back, pummeling him with her fists. "Let him go!"

His forward momentum never ceased. He threw Mikey into the back of the SUV. With one strong arm, he reached back and yanked Viv from his back. "Boss?"

"Bring her," came the barked command. "Hurry!"

Shock siphoned the blood from her brain. She'd heard that voice before. Had heard an imitation of it come out of her son. Familiarity niggled at the back of her mind, but she couldn't put a face or name to the voice.

Violently, she was thrown into the vehicle. She landed painfully, half on the seat and half on the floor. She quickly righted herself and folded a suddenly-docile Mikey into her arms. He was obviously terrified. A darkened glass partition between the front and back seats kept her from seeing who was in charge.

But she didn't have to see the man in the front seat to know Steven's killer had captured them.

All was lost. She'd put Mikey through all of this only to end up right back where this whole nightmare had started.

ELEVEN

Raw and primal desperation flooded Anthony. He had to stop them from taking Viv and Mikey away from him. Quelling his panic he raised his weapon and sighted down the barrel, aiming for the back tire. His finger squeezed the trigger. The SUV swerved. The bullet hit the rear wheel well. A cry of impotent fury burst from him. He sent another round into the taillight. Tires squealing, the vehicle rounded a corner then disappeared out of sight. Anthony fell to his knees in overwhelming anguish. He'd failed.

Behind him sirens wailed as the scene filled with police and Secret Service agents. Useless.

Especially him.

"We'll find them," Joe said as he put a hand on Anthony's shoulder.

Anthony flinched; he hadn't heard his

brother and Barb approach. This was his fault. They were gone because he'd let his emotions get in the way and cloud his judgment. He never should have allowed her or Mikey to be exposed. He should have foreseen this scenario.

Failure choked him. He couldn't speak to his brother's assurance, couldn't put voice to the fear that he would be too late if he did find Vivian and Mikey. He'd botched the most important assignment of his life. To protect the woman and child he loved.

He dropped his face into his hands as the truth spread through him. He loved Vivian. With a love that defied reason.

He'd started out prepared to not like the beauty queen, had in fact at first considered her a spoiled woman who'd thought she could get away with murdering her husband. But Viv had turned out to be so much more than he'd even dreamed.

Kind, courageous, intelligent. A woman to be admired and respected. A woman who loved with a fierceness that Anthony longed to have directed at him.

This emotion, this love, was so different than what he'd felt for Becca. They'd shared a comfortable, easy kind of relationship but he'd never felt the urgency, the passionate need to bind himself to her. Not the way he did with Viv. With Viv he wanted to jump into the relationship with both feet and face the future together.

His hands fisted. He lifted his gaze heavenward. Rage filled him. Words of anger and blame surfaced and lay trapped on his tongue. *Why! Why did You let them take her away from me?*

Viv's words came back to him once again, spearing his tortured soul.

It's convenient and easy to blame God.

The truth in her wise words resonated with him now like never before. Putting the blame on God kept Anthony from facing the truth.

He was the one to fail, not God.

Guilt, ugly and harsh, reared up and stabbed him.

The Kashmir delegate. Anthony had hesitated when he'd seen the gunman aiming at the man he was protecting. For that split second he'd remained frozen, not believing what he was seeing. And that had been all it had taken to end a life.

A new guilt sliced through him, leaving gaping wounds in its wake. Viv. Mikey. He'd let them down. He hadn't kept Viv or Mikey safe from the killer. Now they were lost to him. She was lost to him. Another life, two lives, in jeopardy of ending because of him.

I cling to Him.

So much courage, so much faith in her conviction. He wanted to be like her. To have the same strength of character, the same depth of faith.

A deep-welling need rose and wouldn't be denied.

Oh, please, God in Heaven, forgive me. Help me find them before it's too late.

The prayer rose from his soul, releasing the strangling guilt. Determination shoved aside the self-pity trying to overtake him.

He pushed to his feet, his mind working all the angles. He had to find them. He couldn't give up. Wouldn't give up. Viv was a fighter. He had to fight, too.

Yanking his cell phone from his pocket, Anthony called Trent Associates. Lisa answered on the first ring.

"Carlucci here. I need to speak with Simone or James."

"Neither one are here. I can patch you through to Donavan Cavanaugh."

Anthony's hand tightened around the phone. "Fine."

A second passed before a man came on the line. "Hey, Carlucci. This is Cavanaugh. James and Simone are on their way to D.C. as we speak. Their landing estimated time of arrival is ten minutes."

Surprise washed over Anthony. He hadn't expected James himself to join the ground troops, but he was grateful. "I need the contents of a file I sent to James and the list I sent Simone."

"They're bringing them. Can you get to the South Capitol Street Heliport?"

"I'm on my way." He hung up and relayed the information to his brother.

"We need new wheels," Joe pointed out.

Anthony's gaze searched for available transportation. "Come on."

He took off running toward a Suburban parked behind a police car. As Anthony approached, a man disengaged from a group of uniformed officers and waylaid him.

"Carlucci! What do you think you're doing? First you break protocol and evade your team. Now you're involved in a shootout?"

"Gorman, I need you to put out a 'Be On the Lookout' on that SUV."

Agent Gorman frowned. "Already done."

Thankful for that small favor, Anthony pointed to the brown Suburban. "Yours?"

Wariness entered Gorman's hazel eyes. "Yeah."

Anthony grabbed him by the arm and led him to the vehicle. "We need it."

Gorman jerked out of Anthony's grasp. "Why?"

"I'll explain on the way," Anthony said and yanked open the passenger-side door. "Let's go!"

"On the way where?" Gorman hesitated only a moment before hurrying to the Suburban. He climbed into the driver's seat. Joe and Barb slid onto the backseat. Gorman spared them a glance. "What's she doing here?"

"She's with me," Joe stated firmly.

Impatience and fear knotted Anthony's stomach muscles. "We've got to get to the South Capitol Street Heliport. Now!"

Gorman started the engine, shifted the vehicle into gear and took off. "Okay. Explain."

Feeling each second ticking by in agonizing slowness, Anthony gave his former coworker the details. Emotion clogged his throat when he talked of Viv. He cleared his throat and tried for a detachment that wasn't anywhere to be found.

Gorman glanced back at Joe. "How is ATF involved?"

"ATF isn't. Just me helping out my brother."

Taking the streets at a fast pace, they reached the heliport just as a black chopper with the red Trent Associates logo painted on the door flew overhead and hovered to a landing on the flat blacktop.

Anthony jumped out, not waiting for the Suburban to come to a full stop. The information Trent carried could be the only way for Anthony to find Vivian. Pressure built in his chest as he ran out onto the blacktop, ducking low to avoid the rotators. Debris and dust swirled in the air from the blades.

Shielding his eyes with one hand, Anthony yanked open the helicopter's door and reached in to help Simone climb out. She wore black pants tucked into tall black boots. A black duster flapped against her legs. Kyle climbed out behind Simone, looking so grim Anthony hardly recognized him as the same jocular guy he'd met less than a week ago.

James Trent jumped out last. He carried a metal briefcase in one hand. Exuding frenetic energy, he gestured for Anthony to follow him to the large square hangar just off the landing pad.

Once they were situated in the passenger lounge of the hangar, Trent removed the file and Viv's list of names from his briefcase along with a slim laptop. He spread them out on the Formica tabletop.

"It's a good sign they were taken rather than mowed down in the street. Though why the change in M.O..." Trent's expressive face showed a lively intelligence as he contemplated his own words. "It's becoming personal. Our unknown subject wants the honor of killing them himself."

Sharp daggers of pain pierced Anthony. "It has to be someone on these lists."

He hated how desperate his voice sounded, but he couldn't control the tide of dread filling him. Every second brought Viv and Mikey that much closer to death.

"We've narrowed it down to three. Senator Harold Braverman from Kentucky," Trent read off the names. "Lobbyist Marshal Kent and Congresswoman Rita Alavarez from Ohio."

"We can rule out the congresswoman," Anthony stated.

Trent raised an eyebrow. "Do tell."

Anthony recounted Mikey's imitation of the voice he'd heard the night his father was killed.

"But could that voice belong to someone close to the congresswoman? Someone who's using her position to further some unknown agenda?" Simone asked.

"It's possible," Anthony conceded with rising apprehension. Finding the person whom Mikey heard was tantamount to finding a piranha in the ocean. The scope of where to look was vast, with too many variables.

Joe pinned Anthony with a look. "If *you* heard the voice, based on Mikey's impression, would you recognize it?"

"Maybe. I'm not sure." He'd only heard the imitated voice once, and briefly at that.

"It's worth a try," Trent stated, his fingers clicking on the keys of the laptop. "Okay, here we go. Senator Braverman." He turned the screen so it faced Anthony. "Gotta love YouTube."

The screen filled with a tall, gangly man addressing what appeared to be a town hall meeting. The baritone voice spoken in a distinctly country twang wasn't the voice that Mikey had imitated. Anthony shook his head in disappointment and frustration.

Trent turned the computer back toward him

and clicked the keys. "I'm going to assume that hearing the Congresswoman won't help, but if we can rule out the lobbyist then we'll start combing through the congresswoman's life." A frown creased his forehead. "Hmm. Our lobbyist doesn't appear to have any video uploads."

Kyle held a smart phone in his hand. "I've got his office number here." He dialed and asked for Mr. Kent. A second later he hung up. "Mr. Kent is away from the office. And no, Miss Snotty on the other end wouldn't give out her boss's whereabouts."

"Is there any way to get Kent's home phone?" Barb asked, then promptly blushed a bright pink.

"Good idea. Maybe his wife will have an idea where her husband can be found," Joe said, his voice warm with appreciation.

Agent Gorman spoke up. "I can get it."

Anthony ran a hand over his jaw. His voice shook with dread. "That will take time getting through the necessary red tape. Time we don't have."

"I have a contact at the local phone company," Joe offered. "Let me see if I can get her to give me the number."

Barb blinked. "Her?"

Joe raised his eyebrows. "Jealous?"

Making a scoffing noise, she made a face. "No. Just find my friend."

Nodding, Joe moved away to make his call.

Edgy with nerves, Anthony said, "This is taking way too long. They've had them for almost thirty minutes."

Simone placed a cool hand on Anthony's forearm. "I know you feel responsible, but you have to set that aside. Mrs. Grant needs you to stay focused."

"Easier said than done," he shot back. "I screwed up."

She withdrew her hand. "Believe me, I know the damage guilt can do."

Her eyes took on a faraway, haunted expression. He believed her. She carried a burden of her own. Empathy tightened his chest.

"Got it," Joe said with triumph. He held out the phone. "Just press Send."

Anthony pushed the button and brought the phone to his ear. The line rang for several moments before clicking to voice mail. A man's voice spoke. The hairs at the back of Anthony's neck rose. This was the voice Mikey had imitated. He was sure of it. "It's him."

"Marshal Kent, born in West Virginia," Kyle read from his smart phone. "Graduated from Dartmouth. Married to Millie Kent and resides with his wife in Georgetown. Works for the Barrister Group."

"They've been in the news lately," Barb said. "Something to do with defense contracts and the Middle East."

Gorman scowled. "Nasty business, that."

"How do we find him?" Anthony ground out, feeling the seconds ticking by like lashes from a whip.

"Let's start with his assistant." Trent spun the laptop so they could see the image of a well-dressed young man on the screen. "Wendell Brooks."

Wendell sat on a stool near the window of his favorite java joint enjoying a midmorning pastry and a double nonfat vanilla latte. Suddenly he felt exposed sitting in his usual spot. He glanced around, searching for the cause of the unease slithering down his spine. For the past several minutes he had had the distinct impression he was being watched. There was nothing concrete he could point to that made the fine hairs on his arm raise with alarm. And no one appeared overly interested in him.

Still, the sensation persisted.

Sweat broke out on his brow. He tugged

at the collar of his starched white dress shirt and told himself he was being paranoid. Just because he swam with sharks didn't necessarily mean he'd get eaten. Though…the way Kent had looked at him last night, like he was worse than gum stuck to his shoes, had sent a chill of unease sliding over him.

When he'd arrived at Barrister Group and learned that Mr. Kent wasn't in yet, he'd taken advantage of the boss's absence and split. Mr. Kent was a stickler for promptness and hard work.

But when the boss is away, the minions will play.

Kent was always pontificating. *You don't get to be where I am in life without putting your nose to the grindstone and doing the hard work necessary to make it happen.*

Wendell rolled his eyes as the remembered words rang hollow inside his head. Like Kent ever did his own dirty work. A hired team of unsavory characters always got the seedier jobs done. Wendell hated dealing with them. Crude and rough men who eyed him like he were a tasty morsel to be chewed up and swallowed.

But Kent paid Wendell well for his organizational skills. And his willingness to keep his boss's unpleasant secrets.

Secrets that could put them all in jail for a very long time.

If it weren't for the money and the debts piling up, Wendell would walk away.

He shivered. There it was again. That strange, frightening sense of observation.

Not good. Best get back to the office where he'd be safe inside the secure building with the armed guards who weren't on Kent's payroll, and Wendell would know since he handled all the books for Kent. With shaky hands, he gathered the remnants of his treats and threw them in the trash. Pushing through the glass door leading to the street, Wendell was struck once again with the disagreeable feeling of having his every move kept track of.

A mixture of tourists and businesspeople crowded the sidewalk. But none were *looking* at him. Jockeying his way through the throng, he reached the far corner of NW G Street and waited for the light to turn green. When the light changed, he stepped out into the road.

A shudder shimmered over his flesh. Something wasn't right. He glanced behind him with a sense of dread. A hulking bald man with bulging muscles beneath a black T-shirt dogged Wendell's steps.

One of Kent's hired thugs.

Fear rocketed through Wendell's heart.

He increased his pace, eager to reach the sanctuary of their office with its state-of-the-art security system and armed guards. Dodging an older couple holding hands, he hurried for the sidewalk.

Wendell glanced back again. The Hulk closed in. Something shiny glinted in his beefy hand. A knife. A tight fist of terror closed around Wendell's throat.

Panicked, he broke out in a run.

Feet pounded on the sidewalk behind him.

Up ahead a tall, dark-haired man blocked the entryway to the building. He stared at Wendell with a strange look on his face as if he couldn't believe what he was seeing. A grown man in a panic.

As Wendell slowed, he realized the man's gaze went past Wendell's shoulder to his pursuer.

"Hey!" the guy in the doorway roared. "Stop!"

He pushed past Wendell as Wendell pushed to get into the building. Another man, similar in looks to the taller one, raced to get by, too.

Wendell spun around to see Mr. Muscles turn and flee down the street. He hopped into a waiting sedan and roared away, weaving through the southbound traffic, leaving his pursuers in the dust.

Blowing out a breath of relief, Wendell straightened his tie and tried to calm the frantic beat of his heart. He was safe. But deep down he knew this was only a momentary reprieve.

The game had changed.

Obviously Kent had sent one of his minions to do away with him. Anger stirred beneath the pervading fear. After everything he'd done for Kent. The risks he'd taken….

Wendell seethed.

If Kent thought he'd be so easily disposed of, he had another thing coming.

"Wendell Brooks?" a deep voice spoke near his ear.

Startled, Wendell whipped his attention to a stocky man with graying hair and an off-the-rack brown suit. He flashed a badge. "Agent Gorman, Secret Service. May we have a word?"

For a second Wendell contemplated running again. But then he noticed the agent wasn't alone. And the two men and two women looked ready to eat him alive. No way would he manage to evade them all.

Putting on his most practiced smile, he said, "Agent Gorman, what can I do for you?"

A hand grabbed him powerfully by the neck. A surprised cry escaped as he was spun around to find himself staring into the feral gaze of the tall, dark-haired man.

"Where's Kent taken her?"

TWELVE

Trapped in the SUV speeding along U.S. 29 away from the city, Viv waved and gestured to passing cars trying to gain someone's, anyone's attention. But no one noticed. She wanted to scream with frustration. The dark-tinted windows kept her hidden from vehicles sharing the road.

She yanked on the door handle. Locked. With frantic fingers, she worked the lock mechanism. No help there. The driver must have engaged the child-safety locks.

Despair threatened to rob her of what little strength remained. She tried to stay positive. Anthony would come after her.

But for all she knew Anthony was dead.

Grief welled up, filling her eyes with tears.

She and Mikey could be next.

No! She couldn't go there.

She pressed a hand to her forehead. *Stop*

it! she commanded herself. *You can't give up hope.*

Her faith wouldn't let her lose hope. God was on her side.

Shaking with icy terror, Viv clutched an agitated Mikey to her as the SUV turned off the highway and entered the Rocky Gorge Reservoir area and bounced along an unpaved rural road. The wooded areas along the Patuxent River were perfect for dumping a body. Two bodies. They wouldn't be found for a very long time. She shuddered with dread.

Squeezing her eyes shut tight, she chanted in a soft voice, "I will not be afraid. I will trust in the Lord."

Lord, if it is our time to go to heaven, please let it be quick.

She didn't want Mikey to suffer.

The vehicle hit a hole. The SUV jolted, sending a painful recoil through her. She cried out. Mikey's high-pitched wail reverberated through the interior.

"Shut that kid up!" the passenger in the front seat shouted.

Viv sent the stranger hidden behind the tinted partition a caustic glare.

Soothing a hand down Mikey's back, she whispered, "Shh now, baby. We'll get through this, baby."

The SUV slid to a halt in a clearing, the sound of loose rocks and dirt beneath the tires as ominous as a scream. All around them were woods thick with trees and underbrush. All around them were possible grave sites. Her breathing turned shallow with fright.

The men climbed out from the front seats. The lock popped on the side door. Sheer black terror crashed through her like an angry bear disturbed from its sleep. She lunged for the door handle, wanting, needing to keep the door closed and the evil men away from her son. But her grip was no match for the strength of the driver.

The door was wrenched out of her grasp. Viv scooted back and flung her arms around Mikey, shielding him. He squirmed to be free.

Rough hands pulled Viv and Mikey from the SUV. They landed in a heap on the hard ground. Mikey immediately jumped to his feet and began flapping his hands near his ears. His wails filled the sky. Viv stared at the man who'd driven her here. He'd removed his mask, revealing a scarred face and closely shaved scalp.

"Bring them," Steven's killer said from around the front of the SUV.

The driver yanked her to her feet. "Get up!"

No. She wouldn't make this easy for them. She went limp.

With an oath, the man's fingers bit into her flesh. His big hand squeezed her arm in a painful vise. Dragging her behind him with one hand, he easily lifted Mikey up by the waist and carried him.

"Please, don't do this!" Viv pleaded.

The man ignored her and continued on. A handgun was tucked into the waistband of his pants over his kidney. Viv twisted and turned, trying to reach it. Her attempts fell short. Frustrated, she screamed. Maybe someone would hear. Startled birds flew from the tops of massive oak and hickory trees.

"Shut up!" her captor snapped.

Viv screamed louder, giving voice to the fear and anger and despair welling up inside. Mikey, obviously upset by his mother's cries, released his own wild screech.

There was a barely-discernible path through the underbrush. Viv dug in her heels. Mikey wiggled and squirmed. But they were no match for the man who held them. He stopped at a small wooden lean-to. The door stood wide open.

Viv grabbed the doorjamb and hung on. Mikey was thrown inside. The man lifted Viv off her feet and unceremoniously dumped her on the floor.

He gave her a vicious kick in the side. "That's for being so difficult."

Pain exploded throughout her torso. She doubled up with a moan.

From the shadowy corner, Steven's killer tsked. "Really, Carl. That wasn't necessary."

Carl grunted, slammed the door shut and leaned against the wall.

Viv roused enough from the blow to her side to jerk her gaze across the one-room shack.

A man dressed in a gray three-piece suit sat at a small table. Close at hand lay a large-caliber handgun. Astonishment drained the blood from her head. For a moment the room tilted. Black spots burst through her vision. She blinked until they cleared.

"Marshal?"

His lips spread in a semblance of a smile.

Viv trembled at the coldness in the blue eyes staring at her.

"You've made things very difficult, Vivian."

Her mind reeled.

Marshal Kent was Steven's killer!

But the Kents were nice people. Family friends. Marshal had been a mentor of sorts to Steven over the years, always quick to bolster Steven's ego with encouraging words and wisdom.

And Millie, Marshal's wife, had often sought Viv out at social functions. She'd recently asked Viv to serve on a charity's board, raising money for unwed teenage mothers. Viv had had to decline because of the time commitment. Millie had understood.

Which explained how the men hunting them had known about Mikey's Wanderer Alert system.

Viv struggled to an upright position. Mikey had quieted and stood in the opposite corner, rocking slightly as he twisted his finger.

"Why?" she asked, her voice revealing her astonishment. "Why did you kill Steven?"

Kent blew out a breath. "Believe me, Viv, he didn't have to die. He was one stubborn man. I tried to talk some sense into that boy, but he wouldn't listen." He gave a mournful shake of his head. "I taught him so much. Poured myself into him and his career. And then he turned on me. I couldn't allow that."

Somewhere between her curiosity and her fear was the thought, *keep him talking.* As long as he wanted to talk, he wouldn't kill them. "You were part of his straw donor scam. He was blackmailing you."

"Clever girl. Only he wasn't the brain-child behind our own personal little hedge fund. I was," he boasted with pride. "I needed him to win the upcoming election. There are plans that need to be fulfilled. Steven was the golden ticket to making everything possible." His face twisted in a dark rage. "Now I'll have to start over. Groom some other schmuck. It isn't as easy as it used to be. Too many watchdogs now."

"So Millie was a part of this scam?" Viv said. "Her kindness toward Mikey and me was all a pretense?"

"No, no. Dear, sweet Millie has her head so high in the clouds she doesn't know which way is up." He pushed to his feet.

Panicked, Viv stalled. "Why Steven? How did you pick him?"

Marshal raised an imperious eyebrow. "I didn't pick him. Your father did."

Shock clutched at her chest. "My father?"

"Didn't know we were acquaintances, did you? Yes, your father had a vested interest in wanting a political figure in his back pocket. He discovered Steven. Even financed Steven's first campaign. But then Steven turned on him." Again, Marshal shook his head. "I should have anticipated Steven's betrayal."

Mind reeling, Viv said, "I don't understand. What do you mean Steven turned on my father?"

There had always been an undercurrent of tension between her father and Steven. But she had dismissed the unease as her imagination. After all, her father had advocated the strongest for a marriage between his only child and Steven. Her mother had run a close second. Her mind grappled with the revelation that her own father had used her for his own gain. What kind of parent did that?

Viv glanced at Mikey, longing to take him into the shelter of her arms. The more Marshal spoke the more withdrawn Mikey became. He had sunk to the floor and hugged his knees to his chest. She ached for her child.

"Your rascal of a husband threatened to expose your father's less-than-ethical land deals. All LeMar had to do was persuade you to become Steven's bride. Which I could appreciate. A smart move on the boy's part. Steven wanted the validity your family name and money brought with you. Plus having a former beauty queen on his arm didn't hurt any."

She'd always known she was nothing more than a trophy wife to Steven.

Marshal gestured to Carl with his hand. "Take care of them. There's a shovel behind the hut. Bury them deep."

Carl straightened and moved toward the corner where Mikey stood.

Terror jackknifed Viv's heart. She bolted to her feet and rushed to her son. Pushing him behind her, she implored Marshal to reconsider. "Please. Please, don't do this. I can keep your secret. Mikey can't even tell us what he saw that night. There's no reason to kill us."

Marshal's expression showed a flicker of regret. "Sorry, dear. Too many loose ends."

Desperation clawed at her throat. Beyond Marshal's right shoulder, movement outside the window momentarily snagged her attention. She had to be hallucinating. She thought she saw Anthony peek over the windowsill. Everything inside her stilled for a heartbeat. Hope zoomed through her bloodstream. Her faith in God, in Anthony, hadn't been in vain.

Frantically she sought to give Anthony and herself more time. Holding Mikey tightly in place behind her, she pleaded, "Wait. Please tell me why my father picked Steven. What was so special about him?"

Marshal cocked his head to the side and studied her. She forced herself to return his gaze while keeping her face as neutral as possible.

Finally he said, "Steven could move a crowd to tears or to laughter easily. He made people trust him, believe in him without any concrete reason for doing so. All the best traits of a good politician. He caught your father's attention when he ran for the Boise City Council. The rest, as they say, is history." He gestured to Carl. "And so are you."

Carl raised his weapon.

Viv screamed, "No!" She flinched expectantly, then pulled Mikey down into a crouch. His terrified screams bounced off the wall.

The door burst open. Two successive gunshots rang out, reverberating within the confines of the shack. Carl hit the floor with a cry and a clatter, his gun sliding from his slackened fingers. He grasped his thigh with one hand where blood flowed from a gunshot wound. He held his other arm to his chest. Viv could see another bullet wound in his forearm.

Standing in the doorway, Anthony lowered his weapon. His ragged gaze locked with Viv's. Her heart leapt. She nearly collapsed with relief as love for this man, her hero, swamped her. In two long strides he was at her side, reaching to help her and Mikey stand. Mikey's cries quieted at Anthony's touch, solidifying how much the boy had come to love Anthony as well. Viv couldn't think of anyone she would want her son to love more than Anthony.

Other men filed in. Joe and three others she didn't recognize. Marshal backed up until he was standing beside the table.

"It's over," an older man said as he moved toward Marshal. "You're under arrest, Kent."

Viv caught Marshal's slight movement as he reached for the weapon lying unnoticed on the table.

"Gun!" she yelled.

Anthony shoved Viv and Mikey behind him and whipped around, his own weapon already coming up.

Viv held her breath.

Marshal froze, then raised his hands as several other weapons were aimed at his chest.

Relief bowed Viv's head. Once again Anthony was willing to risk his life for her. He was a man who would always risk his life for others. She knew it and accepted it. And loved him all the more for it.

Viv watched with satisfaction as Marshal was cuffed and escorted from the shack, a man on either side of him. Joe and a blond-haired guy carried Carl out the door.

Anthony heaved a sigh and tucked his weapon into his holster.

Needing to reassure herself he was real,

Viv reached up to caress his face. Tears of relief and joy rolled down her cheeks. "You're here. How did you find us?"

"I'm here." He turned his face to press a kiss to her palm. "Kent's assistant told us about this parcel of land and the shack. It seemed the most likely place he'd bring you." Residual grief etched lines on his face. "I'm just so glad we arrived in time."

"Me, too."

With a look of tenderness and pain, he bent his head and captured her lips.

She clung to him, the heady sensation of being kissed like she'd never been kissed before making all her nerve endings sing.

A small body forcibly wedged itself between them, breaking the kiss. Mikey threw his arms around Anthony's waist. Viv's heart melted with love for this man.

Anthony gave her a crooked smile. "Come on, let's blow this dive."

Happy to put this nightmare behind her, she smiled. "Gladly."

Viv took a step toward the door and halted. She had to know. "What now?"

"Kent goes to jail. You and Mikey are free to live your lives."

"No, that's not what I mean." Unsure how to ask the question burning in her heart, she bit her lip. The moment stretched as their gazes held.

"They're waiting for us," he finally prompted.

He wasn't going to make this easy for her, was he? Swallowing back her trepidation, she forged ahead because once they walked out the door there probably wouldn't be time for them to have a private moment for a while. And she couldn't wait. "I mean, what about us?"

A pained expression crossed his dear, handsome face. "Viv."

There was so much distress in his tone. She didn't understand. He had to have feelings for her. She was certain he did. His kiss told her the story. "Please. I—"

His sharp shake of his head cut her off. "I shouldn't have kissed you. I shouldn't have done a lot of things. I was out of line. Not your fault. Mine." He took a step back. "My assignment is over. You don't need me anymore."

I do need you! her heart screamed. She wanted him in her life. And not as her bodyguard. She needed his strength, his tenderness. His love. But all she was to him was an assignment. How could she have been so foolish to think otherwise?

Hurt welled. Old pain resurfaced. Here she

was again yearning for the love of someone who had no intention of loving her back.

Pride surged, hiding her inner turmoil behind a polite smile. "Of course. Silly me."

With her head held high she wrapped an arm around Mikey's thin shoulders and walked out, leaving Anthony to trail after them.

And her heart broken.

Anthony entered his parents' house and braced himself. The aromas of homemade pasta sauce wrapped him in a cocoon of warmth easing the exhaustion suddenly zapping his energy. He could hear his family on the other side of the living room wall, in the kitchen. His mother's beautiful laugh, his father's deep voice. Angie's smart tongue as she good-naturedly dissed her husband, Jason.

Familial love constricted his throat, part joy, part pain.

He'd spent the past day and a half answering the AAG's questions and writing out his statement of the events of the past week. James Trent had stood by Anthony and Joe, arguing with the AAG on the finer points of law that the brothers had stretched but not exactly broken in their quest to protect Viv and her son. Anthony was grateful to Trent.

The man was a stand-up guy all the way. He'd even told Anthony to take a few days before deciding whether to take a full-time job with Trent Associates.

Anthony couldn't even think about the future without the agonizing pain of loss burrowing to the furthest depths of his soul. His life was empty without Viv and Mikey.

Saying goodbye to her had been the hardest thing he'd ever had to do.

But he'd had to.

Even when he'd known in that last moment inside the shack she'd been about to say something she'd only regret. He'd had to be strong enough to end what never should have started. She deserved someone worthy of her love. Not a washed-up ex-Secret-Service-agent-turned-bodyguard who'd let her and her son get way too close to the edge of death.

He rubbed at the ache in the middle of his chest just as his sister stuck her head around the corner. Her dark curly hair was loose about her shoulders and her lively brown eyes danced.

"Hey, I thought I heard something." She pulled him into a fierce hug. She released him and linked her arm through his. "You're missing Dad's story about Mom's latest mishap at church."

Despite himself, Anthony smiled. His mom was forever doing something comical at their community church, whether asking the pastor a question in the middle of his sermon or pointing out that Mr. Racine was falling asleep again. Her children found her antics hilarious, while the rest of the congregation wasn't as amused. But what could he say. She was his mother and he loved her.

He stepped into the kitchen.

"Tony, my baby," his mother cried and threw her arms around his neck.

If only her hug could make everything better the way it did when he was a kid. He tightened his arms around her. "Hi, Mom."

"Hey, I'm the baby," Angie groused in a teasing tone.

"You're going to smother the boy," his father's deep voice rumbled from his chest.

His mother stepped back with a good-natured huff.

His father breached the gap left by his mother and drew Anthony in for a bear hug. "Good to see you in one piece."

Memories of the car bomb that had sent him to the hospital with a gash to his forehead flashed in his mind. His gut clenched. It could have been so much worse. He could have died. Viv and Mikey could have died.

He sent up a silent prayer of thanksgiving. "Good to be here in one piece."

Anthony shook hands with Angie's husband, Immigration and Customs Enforcement agent Jason Bodewell. He and Angie had met while Angie had taken a much-needed vacation in Florida last year. Jason had been on a deep-undercover assignment that Angie, being the tenacious Angie they all loved, nearly tanked. After a rocky start, the two had worked together to bring down a notorious arms dealer and in the process had fallen for each other. Jason now ran tactical out of Boston while Angie worked homicide. She couldn't have found a better match.

Just like he had in Viv.

But it had worked out for his baby sister. She didn't carry the burdens he did.

He would never be blessed with Viv in his life. How depressing.

"Dinner's about ready." His mother wiped her hands on an apron covering her slacks and blouse. Her short brunette hair curled around her face. "We're just waiting for Joe and his guest."

Anthony raised an eyebrow in surprise. Last he'd seen Joe was in the AAG's office day before yesterday. "Joe's in town?"

"Yes, son. And he's bringing a *friend* for

us to meet." His father wiggled his still-black bushy eyebrows. Though his father had suffered a heart attack two springs ago, the old man still had it going on. He'd been a great police officer. Tough, yet fair. Growing up, Anthony wanted to be just like his father, his hero.

Too bad Anthony hadn't lived up to his father's status.

Anthony moved to the sink to wash his hands. He had an idea who Joe was bringing. A pang of longing hit the bull's-eye point smack dab in the middle of Anthony's forehead with a resounding "twing." Anthony wished he himself was bringing a "friend."

Only he wanted more than friendship from Vivian. He wanted to share his life with her. But that wasn't a possibility. And the sooner he got it through his thick skull the better.

The arrival of his younger brother and Barb Jetton distracted Anthony from his own funk. He'd witnessed the attraction between Joe and Mikey's spunky teacher and wholeheartedly approved. They made a great couple.

Joe needed someone who wouldn't take his guff without giving a good dose of it back.

Over the next hour they devoured platters of ricotta-filled cannelloni generously doused with the best marinara sauce in all of Boston and nicely-aged parmesan cheese. Thankfully, Anthony was able to actually relax and enjoy the festive mood.

But always at the edge of his mind was a tortured yearning for Viv and Mikey. And the family unit they would never be together.

After dinner, Joe drew Anthony upstairs to the house's upper deck. Stars twinkled in the heavens like diamonds, making a perfect backdrop for the city. The lit up view of Bunker Hill, a scaled-down version of the Washington Monument, in the distance made Anthony's heart spasm. Memories flooded him.

Viv's wide blue eyes filled with fear. The moment when Anthony had seen the big goon approaching her with his gun aimed at her heart. The joy in her face when she'd flung her arms around Anthony's neck. The softness of her lips beneath his. The hurt in her eyes when they parted.

When he'd sent her away. Acted as if he didn't love her.

He spun away from the view and plopped onto a lounge chair. The outside house lights cast shadows over the deck.

Joe loomed over him. "Dude, what are you doing here?"

"Excuse me?"

Taking a seat next to him on the other chair, Joe gave him a hard stare. "You should be in D.C. with Vivian."

The bald statement sent Anthony's pulse pounding in his head. "She's in good hands."

At least her safety was. But no one could love her the way he did. His shoulders sagged. "I should have taken her straight to the Department of Justice the minute we returned to D.C. They would have done a better job of protecting her than I did. Even she agreed the DOJ was a better choice for her and Mikey's protection."

Joe held up his index finger. "First off, bro, you did your job. You protected her. She's alive and well and the bad guy is going to prison. Yeah, there were some bumps and close calls along the way, but that's life." His middle finger joined his index finger. He jabbed the air for emphasis. "And second, it was your idea to turn her protection over to the DOJ. She trusted you to know what was best for her and her son."

Anthony swallowed the lump in his throat. "I don't think trust had anything to do with it. She thought I couldn't hack it. And she was right."

Joe scoffed. "For a smart guy, you sure

are dumb. She thought no such thing. And I happen to know, since she and Barb talk. You're real good at assuming stuff but you stink at going after the truth."

The barb stung. "Can it, little brother."

Joe leveled him with a challenging look. "You gonna make me?"

Too heartsick to want to fight, Anthony scrubbed a hand over his face. "Just go away."

"No. Your job is not over."

Frustration fractured Anthony's control. "Don't you get it?" he snapped. "She became more than a job. I crossed the line. I fell in love with her."

Stunned to have the confession out, Anthony clenched his fists. His head dropped back against the backrest.

"Have you told her?" Joe asked, his voice now soft with empathy.

"Of course not. The last thing she needs is…me."

Joe punched him in the arm.

"Hey!" Anthony rubbed the spot on his biceps.

"You are exactly what she needs, you idiot."

"My life is here," Anthony countered listlessly.

"Really? Or is that just a convenient excuse?" Joe stood and shook his head in disgust. "I never took you for a coward."

Normally those words would incite a tussle between the brothers. But not tonight. Tonight, his brother's pronouncement punctured a hole through every last vestige of self-respect Anthony possessed. "But that's just it, Joe. I am. I froze." The admission tasted bitter on his tongue. "My protectee is dead because I hesitated."

Slowly, Joe sank back to the chair. "The delegate from Kashmir." He placed a strong hand on Anthony's shoulder and gave a squeeze. "Brother, that doesn't make you a coward. That makes you human."

"A human trained not to flinch. And I flinched."

"We've all done it," Joe said in a firm tone. "Last year when I went down to Loribel Island to bring Angie back..." He let out a soft whistle. "There was a moment when I came face-to-face with my mortality. It scared me spitless."

Anthony met his brother's sincere gaze. "No one died on your watch."

Joe's mouth twisted in a wry grimace. "It wasn't anyone's day to die, that's all. But that doesn't mean the next time I'm confronted with a deadly situation I'll be as lucky. All we can do is trust God knows what He's doing and go with it."

I can't let circumstances dictate my faith in God.

Ah, Viv, Anthony's heart cried out. *I wish I had your faith.*

He clenched a fist. He was doing it again. Letting doubt and guilt drive his faith into the ground.

Forgive me, Lord. I will trust You.

How many times could a man ask for God's forgiveness before he felt forgiven?

He figured he'd find out eventually.

But right now he had some unfinished business in D.C.

Aware of his brother's expectant stare, Anthony said, "I do want to go after the truth."

A wide grin broke over Joe's face. "Now that's the brother I know and love."

Anthony just hoped it wasn't too late to claim the woman he loved.

"Soon you can put this whole ordeal behind you." U.S. Assistant Attorney General Kevin Jacobs reached for the statement Vivian had just finished signing. "You and Mikey can start over."

Sitting in the AAG's office inside the DOJ,

Viv gave Kevin, as he'd insisted she call him, a wan smile.

She doubted the memories would fade easily.

Even though it had been three days since she and Mikey had been kidnapped and taken to the shack in the woods, she found herself starting at sudden noises. Worse, she was always quickly hurtled back to that frightening moment when she'd thought for sure her life was ending as she stared down the barrel of Carl's weapon. A shudder swept over her. If not for Anthony...

Her mind shied away from thinking about him.

She didn't want to stir the overwhelming heartache and loneliness that at times threatened to suffocate her. And always brought the burn of tears to her eyes.

Anthony was gone from her life. A fact she'd have to learn to accept, as difficult as that was proving to be. Each night she prayed God would lessen the ache of missing Anthony. Each morning she awoke still hurting. Seemed God was taking His time answering her prayer.

But Anthony had wasted no time exiting her life.

As soon as he'd handed her over to the custody of the DOJ he'd returned to Boston with the Trent people.

His goodbye had been simple, unemotional. Bodyguard to client. Only Mikey had garnered a lingering glance that told her Anthony wasn't as unfeeling as he acted. She decided that look had been for Mikey alone, from a kind man who would miss a cute kid. But Anthony was still falling back on what was safe, what he knew; picking his job over her and Mikey.

Focusing on her son had so far kept the torment of loving Anthony and not having her love returned at bay. She was getting on with her life. Like Kevin had said, a new life.

She'd hardly been able to let Mikey out of her sight. She thanked God every day for their survival as well as Mikey's mind's ability to discard the unpleasantness of the past week. The behavioral specialist Dr. Mason did caution, however, to be prepared for Mikey to recall the violence he'd witnessed.

Barb and Dr. Mason had insisted the best thing for Mikey was to immerse him back into his regular school schedule. She knew they were right. And her dear, sweet Mikey had begun to reintegrate smoothly.

Viv could have easily afforded a new house if she wanted after the one she'd shared with Steven had burnt to the ground. Instead, she'd found an apartment in the same building as Barb, needing to be close to a friend. Though Barb had taken a short trip to Boston with Joe right away. When she returned, it had taken every ounce of self-control Viv possessed not to ask about Anthony.

Taking one day at a time had always been her motto. Even more so now. And writing out the week's events in chronological order along with Marshal's confession had been cathartic in some ways. But she was also reminded how brave and heroic Anthony had been.

"What will happen to Marshal?" she asked.

"He'll be indicted and prosecuted for murder and a variety of other crimes," Kevin replied, taking his seat in a high-back presidential chair behind a solid wood oval desk. "His assistant Wendell Brooks pleaded out for a lesser sentence in exchange for incriminating evidence against his boss. Wendell kept meticulous records of all of Mr. Kent's dealings as well as taping several of their conversations."

"Poor Millie." Empathy squeezed Viv's heart.

She could only imagine how devastated

Marshal's unsuspecting wife must be right now. Viv was still reeling from the knowledge her father had basically bartered her life for Steven's silence. The betrayal cut deep. Somehow she'd have to find the strength to forgive him. God would want her to. She knew the path to freedom was through love and forgiveness.

A knock sounded on the office door.

"Enter," Kevin called out.

As the door swung open Viv glanced up expecting to see Mrs. Olivetti, the AAG's secretary. But the older woman didn't walk through the doorway.

The one man she never expected to see again did.

Viv blinked. The world tilted. "Anthony?"

His onyx-colored gaze met hers. "Hi, Viv."

The uncertainty, the hope and tenderness flashing in those wonderful eyes sent her heart thumping. Every cell in her body jumped to attention. Her hands clenched the arms of the leather chair to keep from bounding out of her seat and into his arms.

"Right on time," Kevin was saying as he rose from behind his commanding desk. "We were just finishing up here."

"Thank you." Anthony stepped closer.

His familiar aftershave teased Viv's senses, making her ache with the longing to nuzzle against his clean-shaven cheek. She'd missed the way he smelled.

Kevin moved toward the door. "Take your time," he said before exiting and closing the door behind him.

Viv's mind scrambled to make sense of the situation. Her heart raced. Her lungs squeezed tight, making her voice sound breathless. "What's going on? What are you doing here?"

"I work here, actually." Anthony took the seat beside her, his knees brushing against hers and sending little tingles bursting through her like Fourth of July fireworks.

He studied her. "You went back to blonde."

Self-consciously she touched the ends of her neatly styled hair. "The black was fading."

"You're beautiful either way."

Her heart hiccupped at the compliment. Warmth spread over her neck and cheeks. "What about Trent Associates?"

He gave a shrug. "They have a great team of protection specialists. And I would have been happy there. But I met someone who made me question my life choices. After some soul-searching, I decided to apply for a job with the DOJ."

Her throat constricted. "You did?"

Gathering her hand, he nodded. "I did. I don't want to risk my life protecting anyone but you. You and Mikey."

As happy as she was to know he wouldn't be in danger on a daily basis again, a jumble of confusion assailed her. "We don't need a bodyguard anymore."

"True." His gaze searched her face. "But maybe you need someone to share your burdens with? And Mikey could use a father figure."

Her bewilderment turned to nervous anticipation. She held her breath, barely daring to believe what her heart was telling her. Or what she was hearing. Her tongue felt thick and uncoordinated. She had no idea what to say.

A tentative expression crossed his handsome face. "That is if you want someone to share your life with."

The vulnerability in his eyes made her want to weep. More than when he told her about being shot. She couldn't bear it. "Anthony—"

"No, please, I want to say this." The intensity in his eyes entranced her. "I love you. I want to spend the rest of my life with you. You and Mikey."

Dizzying elation exploded through her system. Her dreams, her prayers were being answered. For once in her life she was getting exactly what she wanted. It both thrilled and scared her at the same time. Love overwhelmed her. Tears blurred her vision. She blinked them away.

He squeezed her hand.

Pain tempered his gaze. Confusion dampened her happiness.

"If you don't love me, I understand."

Her eyes widened. He'd thought her silence was rejection. She lifted his hand to her mouth and kissed his warm knuckles. "I love you. Without exception. And I would love, *love* to have you in my life for now and forever if you want me."

With a growl of appreciation, he pulled her to his lap and wrapped his arms tightly around her. "Want you? Woman, I can't begin to tell you how much I want you in my life."

She snuggled close, delighting in his embrace. "I'm so glad, Anthony."

As she lifted her lips to meet his, she thanked God above for answered prayers.

Gone was all the heartache and loneliness to be replaced with peace and love.

And a future full of bright possibilities.

* * * * *

Dear Reader,

I hope you enjoyed the first book in the PRO-
TECTION SPECIALIST series. Developing
connected books is always a challenge. But
building a team of individuals dedicated to
protecting others really appealed to me. I
had used Trent Associates in two previous
stories (*Chasing Shadows,* a November 2009
release and *Yuletide Peril,* a 2009 eHarlequin
online read) so expanding the concept into
a series of books, each featuring a different
team member, was a natural progression. I
can't wait to tell more PROTECTION SPE-
CIALIST stories.

Yet, I really wanted to see what happened
to Angie Carlucci's siblings (heroine of *Covert
Pursuit,* a May 2010 release). Combining the
PROTECTION SPECIALIST with the Car-
luccis was the perfect way to fulfill both of
my wishes. I decided to write Anthony's story
because he was the eldest and the one in most
need. Former beauty queen Vivian Grant
turned out to be the perfect match for him.
Each was dealing with some heavy issues
from their past that seemed insurmountable.
Throwing them together and seeing how they

helped each other to grow, to heal and to fall in love was both challenging and rewarding.

As an added bonus, I paired Joe Carlucci with a feisty woman who would keep him on his toes. And you never know, maybe one day we'll see if the pairing stuck.

Until next time.

Blessings,

Terri Reed

Questions for Discussion

1. What made you pick up this book to read? In what ways did it live up to your expectations?

2. In what ways were Vivian and Anthony realistic characters? How did their romance build believably?

3. What about the setting was clear and appealing? Could you "see" where the story took place?

4. Anthony carried guilt for the death of someone he was protecting. How did that guilt affect his life? His relationship with God?

5. Anthony asks how many times he needs to ask for forgiveness before he feels forgiven. What does God's word say about forgiveness?

6. Is forgiving oneself easier or harder than forgiving someone else?

7. Vivian could have let Mikey's autism drive a wedge between her and God but

instead she turned to her faith. Have you had something happen that drove a wedge between you and God?

8. Do you believe that circumstances shouldn't dictate our faith? Can you share a time when you let the circumstances of your life influence your faith?

9. Were the secondary characters believable? Did they add to the story? In what way?

10. Vivian's relationship with her parents was in stark contrast to the relationship Anthony shared with his parents. What kind of relationship do you share with your parents? Your siblings?

11. Did you notice the scripture in the beginning of the book? What do you think God means by these words? What application does the scripture have to your life?

12. How did the author's use of language/ writing style make this an enjoyable read?

13. Would you read more for this author? If so, why? Or why not?

14. What will be your most vivid memories of this book?

15. What lessons about life, love and faith did you learn from this story?

LARGER-PRINT BOOKS!

**GET 2 FREE
LARGER-PRINT NOVELS
PLUS 2 FREE
MYSTERY GIFTS**

Love Inspired®
SUSPENSE
RIVETING INSPIRATIONAL ROMANCE

Larger-print novels are now available...

LARGER-PRINT BOOKS!

GET 2 FREE
LARGER-PRINT NOVELS
PLUS 2 FREE
MYSTERY GIFTS

Larger-print novels are now available...

LILPI IB